The good, the bad and the undecided

A White Fire anthology

Laurie Bell

First published by Laurie Bell in 2020
This edition published in 2020 by Laurie Bell

The good, the bad and the undecided

EPUB: 9781922389091
POD: 9781922389107

Cover design by Red Tally Studios

Publishing services provided by Critical Mass
www.critmassconsulting.com

ABOUT THE AUTHOR

<u>Laurie Bell</u> is the author of the Toni Delle Adventures series for adults (*White Fire*) and the Stones of Power series for young adults published by <u>Wyvern's Peak Publishing</u>. (*The Butterfly Stone*, *The Tiger's Eye*).

A sci-fi aficionado, she maintains an active blog of science fiction, fantasy, and flash fiction pieces at <u>www.solothefirst.wordpress.com</u>, including regular Friday Fictioneers 100-word prompt responses, and serves as a volunteer at her local theatre company, including several stints as assistant to the Director. She has several short stories published in the <u>Antipodean Science Fiction E-Magazine</u> and volunteers as a narrator for the same site.

Laurie lives in Victoria, Australia with her partner and two cats, who have their own mansion just outside.

You can find more information about Laurie and her books on her blog: www.solothefirst.wordpress.com.
You can also follow Laurie on:
Website: www.solothefirst.wordpress.com
Twitter: @Laurienotlori
Facebook: www.faceboook.com\WriterLaurieBell

Dedicated to Gerry.
I love you.

CONTENTS

WHITE FIRE RECAP

Agent Toni Delle always gets her man. Except for one, who abandoned her and then disappeared two years ago.

These days, all she needs is her work. With her partner, a canine robot named Mate, and Zach, her attitude-enabled shipboard Computer Intelligence Interface, Toni is now older and wiser. But she also has enough trust issues to blockade a planet.

Her latest mission is a doozy: find and stop a deadly new weapon that's being smuggled into the hands of criminals all over the galaxy. And hey, while she's at it, perhaps find the missing weapons designer linked to these shipments.

It's got all the things she loves about her job—danger, mystery, interstellar travel, drinking at dive bars—but also brings back specters from the past. Because her only lead to track down the weapons has been provided by the Smuggler, and now he says he wants to help.

But then again, he's not the only one capable of betrayal.

And while Toni is chasing down leads on Uxt, Midock and Marn … you can follow the stories of the good, the bad and the undecided.

GERGE

LOCATION: Classified

Gerge ran. His chest ached with every inhalation of contaminated air, and his muscles screamed, unused to such physical exertion. Still, he ran, as if the demons from the Xendia-damned fire-pits were at his heels.

The treasure gripped in his left hand felt heavier than it actually was. Perhaps it was the weight of the many lives relying on him to get the truth out.

Fear drove him forward when exhaustion should have broken him. It was not a pretty run by any means, more of a hobbling, galumphing jog. Still, he kept moving. He had to complete his mission.

The dirt road lay ahead, lifeless and silent; the dark, absolute. Two moons and the distant stars were obscured by heavy cloud cover. The heat was oppressive. A storm was coming. Gerge could smell it in the air. There was also a bitter taste of ozone along with the tang of rusted iron and burnt timber in the back of his throat. A glance over his shoulder failed to expose anyone behind him, but they were there. He could feel them gaining ground, and it was only a matter of time before they caught up with him. He'd never find a live terminal. Not out here. Not in the time he had left, the seconds slipping away even as he thought about it.

Desk monkey. Keyboard troll. His kind had many names. Zaambuka had not called him any of those. He'd seen something in Gerge that Gerge had never suspected was there. A good man.

Gerge had denied it until he'd turned blue. He destroyed lives, not saved them. Exposed dirty little secrets and laid bare grubby lies. It mattered not if his victims were angels or demons, he spilled it all. Then Zaambuka found him in his bunker and forced him into the light.

He had regrets. He had changed, become a different man, a better man. He still hunted for secrets to expose but now he did it for the lives he could save. Zaambuka had told him there would be salvation. Gerge had not believed him, but the choice had been to join or be imprisoned for life. The fear of a life without the holonet did what words could not. He'd joined. He'd trained. And then he'd gone to work.

And he *had* seen the light. The first life he saved filled him with a warmth that burned away the darkness in his soul. Pleasure was a drug he couldn't get enough of. Happiness expanded as a gas inside him, leaving him walking on air. The anger was gone. The hatred he'd thought sustained him seeped away. He needed more of the light. To get it, he went to the darkest of places. Border world skirmishes became his hunting ground, where he searched for the ones who gave the orders. The thugs, the guards, the soldiers of fortune, the pirates. The undercover roles consumed his soul. The truth destroyed him. All that was left was for him to die. But not yet.

He had to find a terminal—he had to get the truth to someone who could do something about it. He had to find the light—but where would he find a terminal out here?

Ahead, a shadow appeared, shaping into a ground vehicle as he ran toward it. Then another. Rundown, burnt-out husks lay scattered along the deserted road. Had they been used for target practice? He hoped they had not been shot up while occupied. The heat of the data disk in his palm told him they probably had.

This shooting practice had not been conducted for fun or as a drunken escapade by teenagers too young and stupid to understand what they were doing. The training had a terrible purpose, as Gerge had discovered.

He stumbled down a shadow-filled street of barely standing buildings, the outline of what had once been a vibrant shopping precinct. Was that … a playground? He'd reached the outskirts of a broken city. Maybe he could find a power source somewhere amongst the ruins of this once-thriving metropolis.

A break in the fast-moving cloud cover turned the landscape into motionless monsters. The real monsters were behind him, closing fast. The slaps of his ancient shoes as they hit the road were slowing. Tiredness and his untrained body were giving up on him, denying his mind control over his limbs. The ache in his chest grew sharper and he prayed a heart attack would not take him before he could save his friends.

Friends? Who would have thought he'd find those out here? His team—his contacts—had become his family. Flashes of faces popped up inside his mind. A smile, a laugh, drinking, eating, loving. It was a time of joy and purpose. And then Gerge had found those files, the ones that detailed an attack by an impossible enemy. Delving deeper, he'd discovered altered orders, government patrols redeployed, delivery routes changed that opened gaps in the surveillance. It let something through. Something that needed to silence Gerge before he could report what he'd discovered.

All Gerge needed was time. For that, he had to be out of sight when his hunters drew near. An avian cry, sharp and high-pitched—a laugh of evil—sent shivers over Gerge's skin. He chose the third abandoned home he found and ran inside, sidestepping broken furniture and ransacked belongings. He flipped the closest switch.

No power. *Shenghi!* Keep moving. Don't stop. He tripped over something in the dark. It sent him sprawling to the dust-laden carpet. Plumes of death rose up into the air and up his nose, tickling his brain. A sneeze built. He buried his face in the crook of his elbow as the explosive sound threatened to betray his location. He had to be more careful. To break a bone now or twist an ankle would be the end. He pictured the children, giant eyes and large heads, their pleading voices begging for help. Ollie's look of horror, Vuffa's tears, Mads's anger.

Gerge picked himself up. His pale green hands stained grey with ash and dust. He hobbled through the rear door, shoving between the slats of a broken back fence to reach the next house. It took three more buildings before he hit the prize, the globe above his head sputtering to life, exposing blood-stained blue walls.

Forcing what that meant from his mind, Gerge searched for a working terminal through the shell of what had once likely been a happy home. Broken glass, shattered dolls and torn clothing were all that remained. In the office, he found more broken screens and devices. His dirty fingers scrambled on each one—the slightest spark was all he needed—but it was no use. He'd have to try another house. Gerge was so close to success, he could practically taste it in the pungent air.

A sharp whistle in the distance sent him to his knees. He glimpsed bobbing lights through the broken windows, growing larger as they drew closer.

Too late. You have failed.

Still, he forced his weary body up and bolted down the stairs. The stairs led to a basement. No way out. But there, on the wall … a terminal. The glass display was somehow undisturbed after all this time. It powered up beneath shaking fingers which flew over the detachable keyboard. He thrust the data disk into the terminal dock, grabbed the keyboard and hobbled across the room to scoot under a desk. He could do this next part blindfolded—or crammed into a desk footwell.

His fingers danced, entering command codes he'd long since memorized, before hitting the send sequence with a flourish. *Done.*

He felt it. The warmth filled his blood. Zaambuka had been right. Gerge *had* changed. He saw the light and it was wonderful.

A sharp confirmation beep brought his head up, cracking his skull sharply on the underside of the desk. *Too loud.* Then he heard a different sound, one that flared his nostrils with fear. Boots on the stairs heralding his death.

Gerge made out the whine of a charging weapon, closed his eyes and let himself fall into the light.

STIEV HELKINGTON

LOCATION: The Unspoken Lands

"This is all your fault."

Stiev hissed the accusation at his older brother as they were escorted—pushed—along the endless gray corridor toward Gallian's office. Their usual contact was Dalmith, Gallian's right-hand man. That the boss himself wanted to see them could only be bad.

The oppressive heat from outside had followed them in, and sweat dripped down the center of Stiev's back. This argument had been going on for a while. Kel just didn't grasp how serious the situation was. Gallian did not summon you to his office on a whim.

"Stiev, we're his go-to guys, our shipping routes—"

"*My* shipping routes."

"Yeah, well, your shipping routes are the best, and so are our teams. Even with our low costs, we get the job done. He'll be fine. We just have to explain it was a one-off."

Stiev stopped walking, not even trying to keep the incredulous expression off his face, stunned by his brother's lack of foresight. The Ghil behind them hit Stiev in the back, hard. He jolted forward, glaring at the guard over his shoulder. The beast-like snout didn't hide the sharp-looking fangs projecting from his fat lips. Bloodthirsty and violent, it was not surprising Gallian had Ghil guarding his apartment.

"I was on a winning streak, okay? Look Gallian's cool. He'll understand."

Stiev wanted to clip his brother over the ear to make him see sense. He didn't. Kel would punch the shenghi out of him. And then there was the Ghil behind him. Now was not the time to be physically aggressive. He worried it would only encourage the Ghil to violence. "He won't *understand*. You put the whole project behind schedule. I can't protect you this time, Kel. You can't be so stupid that you don't see that?"

"I don't need you to save me."

"You don't know what you need," Stiev grumbled loud enough for his brother to hear him.

Kel frowned. "You worry too much."

The Ghil shuffled closer and sniffed at Stiev's sweat-soaked collar. Stiev squirmed at the touch of the sticky tongue licking the moisture off his neck. He twitched away and fell against his brother's weedy body, staring back at the Ghil, mesmerized by the saliva hanging from its fangs.

"People who call Ghil ugly have never seen one up close," Kel muttered.

Stiev spied the sweat beading the white skin at Kel's receding hairline. It exposed his true feelings. So, he was worried.

Yeah, this is not going to end well for either of us. Stiev ran his fingers through his own damp hair. The Ghil sniffed at the stink rising from Stiev's underarm, the sound turning Stiev's stomach.

"Moooove." Meaty hands encouraged Kel forward. There was a loud crunch and Kel groaned. Stiev shuffled forward before he received the same motivation.

"You all right?"

"Never better."

The Ghil grinned, slack skin pulling back to expose his sharp teeth, like a picture straight out of a childhood horror story. He chuckled. At least Stiev assumed it was a chuckle. The sound that emerged reminded Stiev of his lightship's generator. He shot a look at his brother, the smirk dancing at Kel's lips said he'd made the same connection. A rare moment of comradery between the siblings.

Delay over, their procession continued down the austere corridor until they were stopped by a sealed door. A beam of light sprang forth from a port in the doorframe, scanning them for weapons, before the door, as thick as the Ghil's arm, swung inward. It seemed that Gallian did not welcome uninvited guests. Stiev swallowed his fear and stumbled into the sharply lit room.

"—distribution made to both locations." Gallian's stare landed on Stiev as they entered, though the rest of his body did not move. He held a commdisk to his mouth—obviously they'd interrupted an important call. The human man examined them with sharp gray eyes and it gave Stiev chills. An expensive-looking dark blue suit did not hide the man's muscular frame—he was clearly a man capable of violence.

This was not how Stiev had wanted to meet their invisible boss. *Khegh it*, he'd never wanted to meet Gallian. Much safer to remain unknown by such a dangerous man and just work through Dalmith. Dalmith had been Kel's idea. Kel's contact. Kel's suggestion. Stiev never should have agreed. But Kel's debts would get them both killed either way. Stiev hadn't argued, though he'd known it was a bad idea. Sell a few of the guns on the side, make a little profit and pay down Kel's recent loss. *Khegh.*

Gallian's gaze narrowed and the hairs rose all over Stiev's skin. *We are kheghed.* Gallian spoke again, his stare not shifting from Stiev's face. "Immediately. Remember to whom you are speaking."

A man of that size should have a deeper voice, Stiev thought. There was a burst of sound from the disk. Stiev couldn't make it out. "Convenient," Gallian said, his voice crisp and cold. "I expect a more favorable report tomorrow. I would not wish to send Dalmith to ease your burden for you." The sounds coming from the communication disk fell silent. "Good." Gallian closed the link and placed the disk-shaped receiver on the desk. He stroked two fingers against his tanned, clean-shaven chin. "Gentlemen."

The Ghil grunted and shook his hairy head, spraying saliva across Kel's back. Gallian's gaze did not waver.

Stiev dropped his stare to the plush red pile of the carpet. Kel shuffled uncertainly beside him.

Gallian sat back, the creak of his chair drawing Stiev's gaze up. Gallian flicked his hand at the Ghil, who took up a position next to the door. A second Ghil stood on the other side of the doorframe. There were no windows this far underground. No other way out of this room. *Not ominous at all.*

"Which one of you boys," Gallian spoke at last, breaking the silence fallen over them, "enjoys a game of cards?"

Stiev's heart rate sprang into orbit. *He knows.* Stiev fought not to glance at his brother, knowing his face would give the game away. Gallian had found out about Kel's side hustle. Stiev knew Kel's grand plan would blow up in their face. *Shenghi.* They were dead. There was no way Gallian was letting them leave here alive.

"Well, ya see, Mr. Gallian, it's like this," Kel said, shooting Stiev a raised eyebrow, grinning his *I got this* grin. Stiev widened his eyes, trying to convey his own *shut up!* stare. Kel grinned. "It's a heck of a wait between shipments and—"

"Did you win?" Gallian's voice was soft. It raised every hair on Stiev's body.

"Huh? Oh yeah, I must be on a streak or somethin', right, Stiev?"

"Sir, we are behind," Stiev said, locking eyes with the man behind the desk. The Ghil chuckled. *Shenghi.*

"And how do you propose to fix that?" Gallian crossed his legs. His fingers tapped steadily on the desk.

"Open a call to the smuggler gangs. They won't ask questions regarding delivery if the price is right," Stiev told him. It was the plan Stiev had already ran past Kel, and his brother had set up several meetings for this week with a number of gangs. Stiev knew it would work to get the shipments back on track, he just would have preferred to have it all in place before Kel told Dalmith. It was better to be proactive in these situations. Shipping delay? Fix it before you tell the boss. They should be talking to Dalmith, Gallian's second in command, as he called himself, and Kel's direct boss. Why the khegh were they here talking to Gallian instead? If Stiev could only stop his brother from jumping in for a second, he could get in front of this disaster. Head it off, so to speak, before the noose swung their way.

"An interesting suggestion." Gallian's stare shifted to Kel. "And is this your proposition too, Mr. Helkington?"

Shenghi. Don't ask Kel.

"Yes, Mr. Gallian. Stiev plans the routes. If he says they can do it and make up the lost time, it'll work."

"I like to gamble, Mr. Helkington, and I enjoy the occasional bet. Do you bet, or is it just the cards you enjoy?"

Shut up, shut up, you neffing khegher. Don't answer him.

"Ahh sure, I bet, if I've got good odds." Kel's panicked stare darted around the room, not stopping on anything for very long. "What did ya have in mind?"

"How much would you like to bet on which brother will leave this room alive?"

Stiev did not take his eyes off the seated man. He was afraid to draw the man's attention to his half-wit of a brother. Inwardly, Stiev sighed. *I'm so sorry, Kel.*

Kel smiled, displaying crooked teeth. "Well, Sir. You need both of us alive because the smugglers are real selective about who they deal with, right? They won't take kindly to new players at this stage in the game." Kel nudged Stiev. "Right, bro?"

"Is your brother right, Mr. Helkington?" Gallian placed his hand on the arm of his chair, his fingers tapping against the padded material. It was not a nervous habit.

Stiev held Gallian's cold stare through sheer force of will, not wanting to appear weak. His body trembled. "Sir, smugglers are paranoid, and they won't work with anyone they don't trust." Damn the quiver in his voice.

"And they trust you, do they?"

"As much as they trust anyone, Sir."

"Do they need both of you?"

Stiev didn't answer.

Kel shifted in the long silence, twitching, finally realizing that the interview had turned. "Now, ah—"

"Mr. Helkington," Gallian said, addressing Kel, "you are quite a confident gambler, however in this case"—he brought his other hand above the desk and fired his pistol—"you lose."

Stiev froze as his brother hit the ground. Burnt flesh seared into his nostrils as Kel's blood splattered the carpet around Stiev's feet. The Ghil snorted and then coughed, phlegm rolling in his throat. The sound grated in Stiev's ears.

Gallian lowered his pistol. "I trust you will keep your word and get the shipments back on schedule, Mr. Helkington?"

Stiev swallowed, his mouth bone dry. Emotion choked him and yet he was able to force out, "Yes, Sir."

Kel stared up at Stiev, his eyes blank. A hole gaped in Stiev's chest—a hole shaped like his idiot brother. *I'm so sorry, Kel.*

"The full shipment must be completely distributed before my project can proceed. Do you understand?"

Stiev nodded.

"You may go." Gallian pointed to one of the Ghil and flicked his fingers toward Kel's body. "Get that out of here."

The beastly man shuffled forward and grunted as he hoisted the body over his shoulder. Blood trickled down the Ghil's back as he lumbered out the door.

Gallian grimaced at the blood soaking into the rich red carpet. He pressed a button on the desk panel. "Get me Dalmith."

Stiev's eyes closed on the red stain. The remaining guard prodded him hard in the back and Stiev allowed himself to be pushed from the room.

*

LOCATION: Jantiea * Bar Five *

Stiev peered around the crowded smoke-filled bar Kel had chosen as the meeting point. Unease pricked at his skin. This should have been his brother's job, dealing with the jump and droppers. Kel's dead stare appeared in his mind. He couldn't rid himself of the memory, and it chilled him to the core. He rubbed his hands together, his skin cracked and red. He just couldn't seem to get warm.

Stiev had already met with the representatives of two other gangs. A tall white-skinned man with long black hair—one of the Trajik—and a woman in a yellow jacket with sharp eyes and gel-like red skin from the Raln. They had both agreed to the mutually beneficial arrangement.

He hated this. Hated going from bar to bar to ensure none of the smugglers realized the others were involved. But he needed ships. The smugglers were notorious for their internal squabbles, and if they realized their access to his cargo was not exclusive, they would bolt, and he'd be dragged before Gallian again—a meeting he'd likely not survive.

Hiring the gangs required a delicate hand. The volatile men and women easily took offense and had unusual personal codes, like refusing to ship class-four weaponry. It was like flying through a Sector-border minefield blindfolded. This next meeting was one of those. A smuggler from the Cross.

As long as the woman didn't open any of the crates the delivery would be fine. It was a risk picking the Cross, but they were the fastest of the smuggler gangs, and fast was what he needed.

The bar Stiev had chosen to meet this particular woman in was one of the cleanest he'd found on this windblown hell of a planet, although that wasn't saying much. Clean was relative.

He had to wrap this up and return to the warehouse to plan the new shipping routes, not waste his time nursing his second shot of Telale gin waiting for a smuggler who was over a standard hour late. But he had suggested using the smugglers to speed up the delivery schedule, so he had to make it work.

"Never trust a man who nurses his drinks." The pale-skinned woman who sat down opposite him placed her half-empty glass on the stained table and stretched out her long, long legs. *Shenghi.* Stiev's gaze ran up over her body, and he had to tear his eyeballs from the skin-tight green shirt unbuttoned halfway down her chest.

"Oh honey, you can look. I don't put them on display to be ignored." The woman grinned at him, flicking long hair of green, gold, lavender, violet and orange over her shoulder. He made the mistake of looking into her eyes. He couldn't tell if she was joking. "Kel, right? Well, Kel, you called this meeting, sweetheart. Are you going to talk or just sit there?" she asked.

Stiev didn't correct her. If she believed he was his brother then there'd be fewer questions about where Kel was. Fortunately, all of Kel's initial communications had been via text. He shook himself out of his daze, "I have a job and—"

"Hush, hun, not so loud," she admonished. Her violet eyes sparkled as though he amused her. He probably did.

He prickled at the thought. "Do you want the money or not?"

She held up a hand. Doing so lifted the edge of her shirt, exposing a white-handled pistol tucked into her belt. "Go on."

Stiev glanced warily around the bar and checked the tables behind him. No one stood close enough to hear them. Still, he leaned forward and lowered his voice. "I have some crates that I need taken to Kyth-tact."

"What's in 'em?"

"None of your concern. They can't be opened—there's a security seal. In order to get paid, the seal must be intact upon delivery." A bottle hit the floor closer to the bar and a peal of laughter came from the woman who dropped it. Stiev glared at her drunken compatriots and hunched his shoulders.

"Sounds simple enough," the smuggler told him.

"You have to make the delivery within 128 standard hours."

"That will be tight." She scowled. Raucous cheering came from the booths at the rear of the bar and from around the Duilk table where one player threw his cards down in disgust. The smuggler grinned at them and raised an eyebrow at Stiev.

"You'll have to leave immediately," he told her.

"Sweetheart, I never said I was taking the job."

He smiled at her then, flashing his crooked teeth. More cheering came from the corner. "No, you didn't." He held out a piece of plastipaper with a unit number. "Pick up the crates here. You get a bonus for every hour you arrive early."

The woman placed her glass down and slipped the plastipaper into her bra. "Payment is made the same way you contacted me."

Stiev nodded. The woman got up and strolled from the bar, getting several whistles and hoots along the way. So much for maintaining a low profile. Stiev watched her every step of the way out and when he was sure she'd gone, he marked off a line in his little green notebook. Three to go, then he could get off this rock and get back to work.

*

LOCATION: Uxt – Gualliun System
As the trucks rumbled from the storage bay, Stiev sighed and rested his hand against the cool glass of the observation window. Giant roller doors closed behind the departing vehicles, rattling the metal so hard it shook the walls around him. The warehouse

was one of the older ones under the complex, located closer to the theme park than the casino. Oil stains coated the walls, leaking down from the levels above. The whole place reeked of sweat and seaweed.

It had taken too many bribes to convince the men to continue working past clock-off. The smugglers were en route, but the final deliveries still needed to be crated up and they hadn't even made a dent in the second warehouse yet. The men were on a break, gleefully shouldering each other out of the way to sit at the table to consume their meager fare. Most of the workers were of human descent, with a few large framed, no-necked Dobers and more Ghil to provide muscle—strong enough to do the work and smart enough to not ask questions.

Stiev winced at the rough laughter that rose up from the table. He preferred paperwork and numbers to people. Conversations were not his thing. Kel had handled all of that and these men knew it. Stiev had no idea how to encourage the teams to work faster.

He glanced out over the empty bay below. An alarm went off at his wrist. He linked it to his tablet and groaned—one of the crates had been opened. He should have known there was something off about that smuggler from the Cross gang.

Yanking his commdisk from his pocket, he initiated the call before he could change his mind. "Sir, we need to send someone to Section 12. One of the pilots is behaving suspiciously."

The angry voice on the other end belonged to his direct overseer. "Why am I cleaning up your mess?" Dalmith growled.

"Better to deal with you than inform the boss of another delay," Stiev said, made brave by the amount of space between him and Gallian's henchman. Still, it didn't pay to make the larger man angry, so he added, "She's easy on the eyes. He'll be pleased if you bring him a new plaything."

Dalmith didn't reply, but hung up on Stiev. Shaking his head, Stiev brought up his lists again. *Could have been worse.*

*

It was worse.

"What do you mean the crates are gone?"

They can't be gone. The bays are secure. It's a kheghing casino, for Xendia's sake, not a border planet on fireworks day.

"All of the crates?" he clarified, glaring at the man who had delivered the bad news. The guard nodded. Stiev swallowed. Gallian would paint his blood across his office walls. This wasn't just a delay this time, the mag-rifles were *gone*. Destroyed. You couldn't make up a shipment that no longer existed.

"Who?"

The guard stepped back. "We have a blurred visual on one of the corridor feeds. Looks like a ghost."

A ghost? Kel come back for revenge? No, it couldn't be. Stiev's imagination was running wild. So, who? Someone out to destroy him. Why? What had he done to deserve their wrath? Stiev spun away from the guard and waved at two of the unwashed, partially drunk workers sitting at the filthy lunch table. "Jimb, Cherly, get out there and find who did this!"

The men didn't budge. They didn't even look up. They just continued their conversation about the shrell races in the lagoon. Same problem as with Kel. More time spent on the races and less on actual work. *Khegh it.* No wonder the packing was so behind.

"Hey! I said *move.*" Stiev approached the table, refusing to back down until the two men sighed, stumbled to their feet and hobbled out through the door. The remaining workers pushed themselves up and Stiev experienced a moment of fear. Then he focused on their faces and realized they didn't want to stay in the break room with only Stiev there for company. Well fine, the feeling was mutual. Shrell-grubbers the lot of 'em. Alone, Stiev slumped into one of the chairs and groaned.

He wouldn't call. His men had time to find the saboteur. If he put in a new order, he could get a second shipment packed with standard rifles and pistols within the day. It would have to satisfy the waiting squads. Gallian wouldn't discover the missing shipments until after the fighting started, and by then Stiev would be long gone.

In the meantime, he'd increase security at the second, smaller storage bay at the other end of the complex. "How did they get into the main hold?" he muttered.

"Stiev, we must get the last of those rifles moving. If the squads don't receive them in time, the entire project will be jeopardized." The lecture came from a reedy voice behind him.

Head snapping to the side, Stiev found his ugly, frill-necked supplier creeping closer on sharp claws. It was only as tall as Stiev's knees and dragged its long limbs forward with each step. *Shenghi.* He'd forgotten the manufacturer was still on site. Stiev bent at the waist and sucked at the air. *Khegh!* "What do you know about the meeting? Why is it so important to the project?"

The Geerp shuffled closer and puffed out its neck frill. "Midock," he rasped.

Stiev dropped his head into his hands and scrubbed his face. A trilling buzz coming from his pocket brought his head up. *Of course he'd call now.* Pushing matted hair from his eyes, Stiev yanked his communication disk from his pocket. "Mr. Dalmith?"

Stiev waved at the Geerp, waiting until the creature limped from the room before he spoke again. "I wasn't aware you knew, Sir—"

"Shut up and listen. Increase your security on the shipments." Dalmith's raspy voice sounded deeper in his urgency. It sent a shiver down Stiev's spine. It was never a good thing when Dalmith brimmed with anger. Thankfully he wasn't here—Stiev would've been his punching bag.

What exactly did Dalmith know? Had he heard about the explosion? *Has he told Gallian?* "I was thinking about—"

"Stop thinking, you fool!" he bellowed. "There's a Protection and Security Taskforce agent on Uxt. Albino woman. Find her, it shouldn't be hard."

Stiev leaped to his feet. *Well, that explains the explosions and the ghost stories.* "Here, Sir?" He lowered his voice. "What do you recommend?"

"Kill her."

"Yes, Sir." Stiev returned the disk to his pocket, pulled his pistol from his belt and ran from the room.

He doesn't know. I can still fix this.

*

LOCATION: Battleship *Capacitor* * Prison Cell 442 *
Dalmith had found out about the explosion and the destruction of the guns. And he wasn't happy.

Stiev's gaze ran around his cell again. He was almost positive he was on a ship, in an onboard brig. He was pretty sure it had been six days—it was hard to tell. He'd been unconscious for a lot of it, or floating in and out of awareness, from his wounds and from what was probably a concussion. The wounds Dalmith had inflicted upon Stiev after his failure to apprehend the Albino agent were gradually healing, his bruises fading. The broken ribs and nose prevented much movement on his part.

His cell was cold and bright, and had two bunks, though he was the only resident. He lay prone on one bunk, the mattress barely an idea.

I'm alive.

Every time the door to his cell opened, he wondered if the Dober with the white streak in his hair had finally come to drag him before Gallian. So far it had only been to deliver what passed for food.

Stiev was frankly terrified he was still alive. It meant Gallian had plans for him. And if that was the case, Stiev would rather be dead.

Yesterday, a great ruckus had sounded in the cell behind Stiev's, the arrival of another prisoner. The vents at the very top of his cell let air and sound travel between them so, after a while, Stiev had struck up an odd friendship with the man. Mostly to relieve his boredom, but also to distract himself from his growing hunger.

"Hey Stiev?"

"Yeah?" he called back.

"You never finished that story, or did I pass out again? You said the agent had found the tablets?" The man's voice had a strained quality to it, much like Stiev's. Probably injured too. He sounded middle-aged and had no obvious accent. Core planet native perhaps? He'd said he was a doctor.

"Yep. She and her men overpowered me. Must have found them after she knocked me out."

"An entire squad of agents attacked you?"

Stiev bit back a moan as he rolled over—the hard surface made his muscles ache, but there was nothing else to lie on—and stared at the wall. A dark brown droplet stained the paint. He imagined other prisoners in this room, ones who'd died in here. Did Dalmith use the cells as his personal anger management program? That was Stiev's biggest fear. Any minute now Dalmith would storm in and finish what he started.

"There had to have been over a dozen of them. They were everywhere." What the other man didn't know, Stiev didn't have to admit to.

"How did you get away?"

"Don't know." That was the problem with a lie. You had to keep track of it. The longer it went on, the more slippery it became.

"And that's the reason you're here now?"

Stiev sat up, stifling another groan. "No, she stole a key that belonged to my dead brother."

"She killed your brother?" The man sounded horrified.

Stiev dropped his gaze and stared at his hands. "No."

"You were betrayed?" The bed in the cell squeaked as the doctor sat down, or maybe stood up.

"Not betrayed. Just used," Stiev grumbled.

A pause. Then, "I've been used too."

"Yeah, well, when I wasn't useful any longer, Dalmith took over." And had kept Stiev alive. *Khegh!*

"Ah, yes. Dalmith. He and I are well acquainted."

"Yeah? Lucky you," Stiev sighed and lay back down again. "Apparently, I was just a diversion."

"I don't understand." The doc grunted. His every movement sounded full of pain. The doc's trip here had clearly been no easier than Stiev's.

"That drug you told me about, Genmiktok, the one you designed?" Stiev shouldn't be telling the doc this, but what did it matter now? He'd been thinking on this for days. It was like that famous magician on Uxt; Kel and Stiev used to go on a good night when the races weren't on. Stiev had taken him primarily to teach Kel how to bluff better. It didn't take. But the thing the magician did well was misdirection. Make the audience look one way while he did stuff with his other hand. "They're gonna use it to poison the water on Marn."

"What?" The doc sounded shocked, angry. Discovering your work was to be used to kill a lot of people had to be a hard truth to hear.

"Yep. The assassination of the Vice-President sets it all in motion. It's Gallian's real scheme."

"Gallian? I've not had the pleasure."

"You don't want it. But, you know, I don't think it's entirely Gallian's plan. It seems, I don't know, too … sneaky?"

"Devious?"

"Yeah."

"I see." There was a long silence and when the doc spoke again, he sounded sad. "That is not what it's supposed to be used for."

"Oh, come on. You made a poison. What did you think it would be used for?"

"Scientific research."

"You really believe that?" The doc reminded Stiev of Kel. High ideals and the lofty belief he was untouchable. It had brought Kel to his tragic end. The doc was in for a rude awakening.

"You said diversion? What was your real purpose?" The doc groaned as he rolled over or sat down again.

"Temporary storage and shipping. Easy to find, easy to get into, even the details for the shipments were faked. We were all expendable. The whole operation was a set-up in case PST found the guns—which they did. So, come to think of it, we … ah … I mean, I succeeded. The assassination covered up the real plan."

"The plan to poison the water on Marn?"

"Yes."

"How did you learn about this?"

"My brother was a fool and a bad gambler, but he had good ears. He told me what he heard and I put it together. Anyway, Dalmith shut the operation down after the agent got away. He, ah, found out the weapon I was to give the assassin, well … the agent got it first. I didn't even know the prototype was gone. Dalmith didn't believe me."

"I'm not surprised."

Stiev sighed. *I'm going to die here. Kel, I'm so sorry.*

"I have the antidote."

"What?" Stiev snapped upright and gasped at the pain that exploded through his chest. His whole body turned cold and clammy as nausea rose up in his throat. He swallowed it back, breathing shallowly through his nose.

"When I devised the poison, I made an antidote. If I could get it to the PST, or to Marn, somehow …"

"How? You're stuck in here."

"I have a plan." The doc's voice cracked as he spoke.

Stiev shook his head sadly. A ridiculous idea. The doc could barely move. No way would he be strong enough to fight. It was iffy to think he stood a chance of surviving, let alone escaping, and Stiev told him so.

"I have to try."

Footsteps sounded, stopping outside their cells. Stiev could hear an argument of some kind and stood up. That was not one of the Dober guards. His panicked breathing was too loud in the otherwise silent room.

This is it. You're gonna die.

Pistol fire, then silence. A loud bang from the cell behind him. *No ... not the doc.* Stiev pressed close to the rear wall, listening with all his might. The doc was coughing and then a voice ... the voice that haunted Stiev's dreams spoke. "Name?"

The doc's voice was weak. "Rober Telksh."

"Doctor Telksh?"

Stiev's eyes popped wide. It was that agent. The one who destroyed the guns on Uxt. He'd recognize that voice anywhere.

"Yes." The doc coughed. "Who are you?"

"I'm one of the good guys. Come on, we need to get you out of here." It *was* her. The agent who had destroyed Stiev's life.

"Wait. There is a poison ..."

"Now's not the best time. Come on, Doc."

A rescue? The doc was getting out. Good for him. Stiev debated calling out, begging to be taken too, but he was sure the agent would refuse. "No, wait, you don't understand ..." The doc tried again.

"Let's just get moving. You can tell me later." That agent was here, and she was rescuing Telksh. Stiev heard another voice.

"Whatcha doing, Toni?"

"Would it shock you to know I was told to find this guy? Help me."

And then … silence.

"Doc?" he tried. There was no answer. Stiev huffed out a sigh and lay down on his bunk again. He didn't blame the doc for getting out and not coming back to help him. The doc was a good guy. Stiev wasn't. Stiev shipped guns—guns intended to kill a lot of people. Besides, he figured Kel was waiting for him.

Gallian would blame the doc's escape on Stiev somehow. Maybe the agent would destroy the ship during her escape. A quick death would be better than what he had to look forward to.

BERNI

Isn't this the life? Berni kicked her booted feet up onto the console and stared around her gorgeous cockpit. Independent. Free. No timesheets or payroll regulations. No shared offices. No spreadsheets. Just open space. The endless dark and the pinpoint light of distant stars to guide her way.

Her cargo hold bulged with contraband. All she had to do was deliver it on time and the massive payday would finally fund her dreams. It was what she'd spent the last few years working so hard to achieve, and now it was within her grasp. Her ticket out. Enough money to purchase a home base, a place to relax—one with a giant walk-in closet and a separate room just for her shoes. "ETA, Dave?"

Her shipboard Computer Intelligence Interface's digital face appeared on the screen left of Berni's elbow. Eyes and mouth only, like one of those emojis the humans droned on about all the time. Dave blinked up at her. "Five standard hours. Like when you last asked."

"Ahhh. Once we make this delivery, Davo, we'll be set. This is it. The big one."

"You will not retire," the CII said bluntly.

Berni yanked her legs off the console and sat up. "Exsqueeze me? That's the plan, sunshine. It's always been the plan."

"You enjoy your work too much to stop. You would grow quickly bored and find a way to cause trouble. The civilian life is not one you are designed for."

"Rude. Yet accurate." Berni stood and pressed her arms high above her head, then stretched backward until her head was level with her butt. Straightening, she pulled one leg high above her waist. "So, what did you find out about our new client?"

"Kel Helkington is dead."

She dropped her leg. "What?"

Dave flashed up an image of an unfamiliar man. "A mugging. Reportedly."

"That's not Kel." She leaned closer, eyes squinting. There was something about man that sent flares up inside her brain. Pale skin, thin hair, and the same chin. "Looks a little like the guy I met, though."

"Kel Helkington did work with his brother, Stiev. Stiev rents a couple of warehouses on Uxt." Another image appeared.

"Oh yeah, that's the guy. Fake Kel. So, real Kel is dead?" She peered over the detritus littering the console. *Hmmm, I should probably clean up at some point.* It was getting a tad whiffy. Take-out containers, empty meal bowls and discarded clothes covered every available surface—floor too. "Why mention the mugging so pointedly, my friend? Do you suspect it wasn't an accidental death?"

"No. The paperwork is in perfect order. Not a single field has been left blank."

"Totally murdered." Berni bent to touch her toes, stretching out her calves.

"Stiev Helkington is not on the holonet much and has no social accounts that I have been able to find."

"A mystery, huh? Interesting. Any hint to what we're lugging?"

"Negative."

"Hmmm." Berni stood to stretch her other leg, pointing her toes to the ceiling. "We could sneak a peek."

"Boss, did not your orders state the crates must be delivered sealed?"

Berni pursed her lips at the screen. "Party-pooper." She could see enough of her reflection to reach for her aerosol lip gloss and spray on a fresh coat of blood red Ruby Delight—her favorite color. "You know things happen on long-haul flights. Accidents and such. Turbulence."

The CII snorted. "In forcedspace?"

"Disturbance in the Ticyons? Unstable flux field?"

"Really?"

"Things happen, buddy. I really think I oughta go down to the bay and confirm everything is okey-dokey."

"And if a crate bursts open while you are down there?"

"Well, then it's a good thing I'll be there to check on the contents. I mean, we wouldn't want to deliver damaged goods, would we? Extremely unprofessional."

"Indeed."

She bent double, grabbing her holsters from the boot well under the console. She pulled both pistols free. Her favorite girls. Eight projectiles each, manual fire, explosive propulsion weapons. Two gem-studded gleaming white handles and two glossy black barrels that had designs on her heart. "Just in case," she said, and winked at the screen.

"Shameless, Boss. You used to have stronger willpower."

"You can't trick me into stalling, Davo. Now, perhaps drop us out of forcedspace. We need a plausible explanation."

"Boss, it is a tight clock."

"Yep, and one little peek won't take long. It'll be fine," Berni assured the nervous CII. Her gaze caught on the holoimage pushed deep behind her plastic Zu Zu plant. Three little heads—hair a riot of color, large lavender-toned eyes and giant toothless smiles—peered back at her. Their silent laughter was trapped in the image, frozen in time. *One day, girls, I'll have a safe place and you can come home.*

She tore her gaze away. "Might be food, huh pal? Fresh balcoke steaks?" Berni sauntered from the Sunchaser's cockpit, tapping her hand twice on the panel above the doorway for luck as she passed under it.

Through the viewscreen the strobing stars outside shifted and froze as the *Tigerforce* dropped out of forcedspace.

*

Berni swore. For a long time. Colorfully. It was actually fairly impressive. She'd have to remember some of those terms for future use. If she had a future.

She stared down at the flashing holonet signal fob wedged in the corner of the crate beneath the strings of packing. The reason she hadn't immediately reacted to it was the items tucked away carefully between the packing strings. Rifles. Dozens of black beasts. When she picked one up, it was heavier than she expected. The strange box where the sight would usually be made her skin tingle. When Dave was unable to determine exactly what it was, the tingle turned into a tremor. She started counting. Each weapon she uncovered turned the tremor into a continual rolling quake that was giving her a stomach-ache, like landing the *Tigerforce* in a snowstorm without any equipment. Or landing gear.

Not a word passed her lips though her mind was in meltdown.

Khegh khegh khegh. Sheghi-loving kheghing cry-baby. Mother of a snark, eating fire and shitting coal.

Then she caught sight of the signal fob. She pursed her lips and tilted her head. "Shenghi."

"Boss. I'm picking up a signal that is—"

"Yeah."

"There's an alert set for when the crates are opened, isn't there?"

"Yeah." The fob shattered prettily beneath her boot heel. "Dave?"

"Get us back in forcedspace?"

"Yea—wait. Put a call through to Colten first."

"Signal is going to be distorted out here. There's a pulsar near—"

"Try it anyway."

Daniel Colten. Her ex-partner. She'd heard he now haunted the systems in this area. Fingers crossed he was close by. She was gonna need backup.

He didn't pick up.

Khegher.

He couldn't still be pissed over that little incident on Tark Seven, could he? She tried him four more times and then left a message. He'd know it was serious because she hated leaving messages. Lifting the rifle so it could be seen on camera, she told him all that had happened as if he was sitting right next to her. "I can't take off and lay low, not with this batch on board." She eyed the stacked crates around her. "Besides, I'd like to know where these creeps got their hands on this kind of modified technology. I mean, there are a lot of crates"—that was putting it mildly—"and they look specially designed. It's not the sort of patch-job you'd see between Sectors."

The better plan would be to make the drop on Kyth-tact and trail the cargo to the next destination. They wouldn't be staying on Kyth-tact. That planet was a shenghi-hole at the rear end of a snapper turtle. "I'll make the drop and put a tracer in one of the crates, work a little magic, turn on a little charm and see what I can find out. If this all goes ass-up, these blokes don't seem the type to accept a written apology, so get your butt here ASAP." Ugh, that had made her skin crawl. The only thing she hated worse than leaving messages was asking for help.

The *Tigerforce*'s proximity alarm exploded into noise. Her eyes darted up, wishing for X-ray vision to see what was going on outside her ship. "Looks like I'm missing a party. Don't let me down, Dan. You owe me." She cut the holonet call.

"Dave?" The ship jerked sideways, as if hit by something, throwing Berni into the side of the open crate and then backward into the wall. If the crate hadn't been tied down, she would have been pancaked.

"It's not so much a party as a raid. You'd better get up here."

"The tracking signal only went off a little while ago. They couldn't have pinged us already," she complained as she ran back to the cockpit. She dropped into her chair and tugged on her restraints. The *Tigerforce*'s engines roared to life—silent in space, but Berni imagined the growl of an ancient Earth tiger nonetheless.

"Perhaps they had someone waiting at the drop zone?" Dave suggested.

A flat-nosed brute of a ship appeared on the display and in her viewscreen. The designation of the ship was *Stalker*. Not ominous at all. And it packed a wallop. Her ship slammed sideways again.

"Where the khegh did he come from?" She fired back, but her ship's shields were taking a pounding. She jerked the stick, fishtailing, doing her best to slip the enemy's firing lock. Her little Sunchaser seemed to screech to a halt beneath her body, slamming her forward. "What else is out there?"

"A class nine battleship."

That awful sliding feeling of a holding beam gripped her stomach. "Shenghi. Picked the wrong time to open the pressies in our cargo bay, huh Dave?"

Berni yanked both her pistols from her belt and checked the clip on each. Full load. Eight bullets each, sixteen shots. Right now, her choice in ancient weaponry was feeling a little like bringing a tissue to a bullock fight. "Bolt the cockpit door. Let's not make it too easy for them and call Jas." Her beautifully beautiful friend and Cross personal assistant answered immediately. Berni grinned. "Dan could learn something from you."

"What? Berni, wha—"

"I'm in a spot of bother, Jas darling."

Jas's caramel-skinned ears flattened to her glossy hair, her eyes widened as Berni was thrown sideways again. "Berni what's—"

Ah, Jas had spotted the girls. Berni raised her pistols. "Yeeaah, it's gonna be a thing. Sorry for flashing the girls at you, hun. Listen, I took a job that turns out was a bad move on my part. Location of the drop is Kyth-tact. The guy I'm working for said specifically to avoid the left ridge. I figure it's a fancy anti-theft thing."

"I'm losing your signal, Bern. Say again?"

"Left ridge. Avoid it. Kyth-tact. I took a peek in one of the crates and disturbed a rattler. You don't have anyone out here, do you?"

"No. Sorry, Berni."

"Put a call out, yeah? Try Colten. I'm sure he's in the area."

"On it. Be careful out there."

The call cut off. Berni didn't think that had been either Jas or Dave's idea. The tugging in her belly stopped and a grinding clank came from the outer room. Her gaze reflexively shot up as the whine and pop of laser fire sounded outside. They'd been towed into docking with the larger ship. Berni glanced down at her pistols.

"They are forcing the hatch." Dave's voice was a spot of calm cutting through her racing thoughts.

"My ship, Dave! I just got her tuned."

"It appears they are fairly angry."

"Wait until they meet me."

"Perhaps next time you should leave the merchandise alone."

"Oh, don't you start."

Loud, violent metal screaming came from the outer room. Dave had sealed the cockpit, but if they could blow the outer hatch, they'd get through this door with no problems. "Let's try Dan again." Berni huffed an unimpressed breath when he didn't pick up and left her ex-partner one last message.

"I have no external signal," Dave told her.

She shrugged. "Keep it in storage with an autosend. You never know, you might get a line out." Berni stared down at her pistols. "It's been a fun ride."

"Indeed."

The cockpit door buckled and groaned. "Shenghi, they *are* pissed." She cocked each pistol and ducked behind her pilot's chair. The protection it offered was miniscule, but she needed the illusion to keep her strength up. Her gaze flicked to the holoimage on the console and she blew it a kiss before turning back to the door and aiming for what she hoped was center mass. Perhaps she should have listened to her CII when he'd said not to open the crates. She thought of the weapons sitting inert but exuding deadliness in her cargo bay ... nah, she'd do it again. Those weapons were not going to be used if she had anything to say about it. "Set off the pulse in the cargo hold."

"Boss, I'll lose every system. I won't be able to assist you."

"Do it. Destroy the cargo. Consider it my last order."

"Boss."

The door shuddered and bent inward.

Bent? *Shenghi, what the khegh is out there?* "Now, Dave."

"Goodbye, Berni."

"See you on the other side."

Every light and hum of power snapped off as the electromagnetic pulse was triggered. Raised voices came from the other side of the door as the lights went dark and everything with power died. A growl became a howl. *Everything* with power, including laser weapons.

Who's got the upper hand now, you kheghers?

Manual weapons, explosive propulsion, metal bullets. Sometimes the old human stuff came in handy. She straightened her aim.

The door shuddered.

"Here we go."

RUMULD

LOCATION: Protected and Sealed

Rumuld had been excited to see what they looked like up close, so it came as a major letdown when the Senator greeted him instead. The weedy-looking man wore his medals and his sash, but the show of power didn't work on Rumuld. Marcus—his brother—had let slip that the Senator had never been deployed. The jeweled wrist chain and rings were an ostentatious show of wealth. Again, this did not impress Rumuld. Family money—the Senator had none of his own. Mommy's pet. Literally. She paraded her Senator son out at every ball.

The excitement of the moment quickly returned as Rumuld was led into the meeting room and he saw the sole occupant. *At last.*

Rumuld stared at the smaller … man? His skin crawled. Humanoid certainly, with weird buggy eyes. Didn't sit right. Same about the hands. They clenched oddly, little finger and thumb moving before the rest. Rumuld was disappointed when the humanoid didn't speak. He'd wanted to know what they sounded like too. *Feck it all.*

He dragged out a seat opposite the Senator. He wasn't supposed to comment on the humanoid. Marcus had drilled those kheghing political lessons into his head over and over. Most of it had leaked right back out. What was the use of it in real life? Didn't help you on the track, did it? Or in the back-rooms? There you only needed money, and lots of it. Still, he remembered enough of the lessons for them to occasionally come in handy. Like now.

Usually, Rumuld didn't care how he stood or how he spoke, for feck's sake. He knew how real men did business. Fermented liquids, cold coin and a guaranteed line of credit. And, in Rumuld's case, a brother who was the Sector President. It opened a lot of doors and, shenghi, it excused almost anything.

Still. He'd come to meet them and had been prepared to play nice. But the Senator had met the watcher first. That's what Rumuld called the humanoid in his head. It meant the Senator had also spoken to the watcher first. That's what manners got you. "But I thought—"

"Did you truly think they came here to speak to *you*?" The Senator sneered. "You are only here because they need to hear the task is done from your lips. It's a little quirk they have. They *hear* the truth." The Senator was from a planet called Jip. His canine like sharp teeth pressed into his thin gray lips doing little to hide his disdain. The feeling was mutual. Rumuld couldn't stand the fecker, but the Jip had been his contact to plan this meeting. Kheghing idiot didn't think Rumuld could talk all political. A kheghing insult was what it was. He knew how to operate. You found out what the other guy wanted and offered it or squeezed it out of him. *Shenghi.* All beings, creatures and monsters alike, had a breaking point. Usually you found it before the bones snapped. Sometimes not.

The Senator was still waffling. "They don't care who your brother is, and they don't care who you are. Their only concern is that their wishes are met."

"Fine." Mangy Jip was looking to get his head punched in.

Rumuld's gaze flicked around the dark, stuffy office. It looked like a room in the back of a club, where the lights were kept low to hide the bloodstains. One door, no wall hangings or doodads. No windows. Just a plain old room with a few chairs and a table. Clearly not a location chosen by the Senator. It'd have more flash and be less work-like. Chosen by their guest, perhaps? If so, they didn't view the moment the way the Senator did—the way Rumuld did. So what did they value? What could Rumuld exploit?

The trip to get here had been a pain in Rumuld's ass, what with all the secrecy. Rumuld glanced at the silent man seated at the table's end. Dude didn't even blink. *Creepy.*

Rumuld turned back to the Senator. "Do you have it?"

The Senator rolled his eyes behind emerald-tinted digital glasses. "It has already been transferred."

"I said it had to be in coin. They'll trace large transfers. It'll look too suspicious." Rumuld rubbed his nose and sighed loudly. "Feck it. I'll have to move it." The Senator never listened. He was worse than a hired goon. Who taught this idiot how to do business?

"Then move it."

The watcher remained silent.

Rumuld inched his chair further away from the silent humanoid. There was something wrong with him, like his skin didn't fit right. Fecker sat as still as stone, pinpoint eyes the only parts of him that moved. They darted from one man to the other as they spoke.

The Senator snapped his fingers in Rumuld's face. "Has it been organized?"

"Yes, yes. Marcus signed the paperwork a week ago." He turned and spoke clearly, slowly, holding eye contact with the watcher no matter how badly he wanted to squirm. The watcher didn't blink, just stared. Rumuld had a sensation of crawling in his nose and behind his eyes, as if the man actually had his fingers inside Rumuld's brain. "The patrols have been redirected and the entire area will be unprotected. Guaranteed."

There was silence as they waited for a response. The watcher jerked his head in a nod. Hopefully his people considered that a positive move. Rumuld turned as the Senator let out a laugh, his body totally relaxed.

"Good." The Senator's tongue lapped at his sharp teeth.

"Are we done?" Rumuld asked, pushing his chair back with his feet. He remained seated.

"Make sure you are not followed when you leave."

Rumuld bit back a snarl. His eyes darted to the watcher before returning to the Senator. He imagined reaching out and strangling the pretentious man. "I always check."

The Senator rose, gathering his dark cloak around his shoulders and raised the hood. "I have a speech to write."

Rumuld glared at the man as he swept from the room. He turned to the watcher. "You think he's an ass too, don't you?"

The man just stared. It was eerie, one eye followed the Senator while the other remained fixed on Rumuld.

Rumuld choked back a nervous swallow and came to his feet. It never did any good to buckle a potential partner. *Don't show weakness.* It was something Marcus should bloody well learn. Failing to show up only ever demonstrated fear, not strength.

The watcher did not move.

Rumuld's hand trembled as he closed his fingers around the door handle. The watcher made no sound. Rumuld tugged the door open and shut it softly but firmly behind himself. Fecking creepy, no doubt.

Once outside the building, Rumuld breathed easier. He glanced up at the darkening violet sky. First sun of the two had already set. Better get moving. He had to return home and move that money before it could be traced. As tension left his body, he slumped into his usual slouch. Inside that room, he'd felt like one of the crocpups his brother hunted, as though a weapon tracer had been drawn on his back the whole time. Out here, the sensation was gone.

He swiped a hand over his sweaty brow. It was all good. Just like at the track. You get a bad vibe, you don't put coin on that race. You hear of a sure thing, you put it all down. And yes—despite the Senator's attitude and Rumuld's bad feeling—this was a sure thing. Marcus wouldn't call him a fool anymore. Rumuld would be a hero. A rich Xendia-damned hero. Marcus wanted the deal done. It got done. He wanted the deal on the quiet. Rumuld had ensured it stayed hush-hush.

Rumuld's position was about to go up. And his first job in the new world order would be to cut that pretentious Senator down to size.

ANTONIO ZAAMBUKA

LOCATION: Sector One Central * PST Headquarters *
"Vice-President Ramo's office, please hold," the pleasant, featureless voice said for what had to be the eighth time.

Antonio Zaambuka was getting the official run-around and he was growing increasingly impatient with it all. The report on his desk taunted him for his lack of attention. This powerplay was beneath him. Procedure, rules, regulations, process. It was all meant to work *for* him, not against him. It was infuriating. Did they not know who he was? The report he had just read raised every red flag he had. Agent Delle's discovery of the holoimages of the Vice-President forced his hand. He'd made the call ... and had been put on hold. He had to speak to the Vice-President now. Not sit here twiddling his toes.

He scanned his office, looking for something onto which he could vent his frustration. However, there was nothing to tidy or straighten. Every folder, tablet and binder was in its place, as it should be. The surface of his desk was completely clean apart from his technology and the classified report. Long practice stopped him running his fingers through his hair; instead he ran a hand over the monstrous human-style tie he wore and released his long-held breath, sucking in another, slowly. Would the Vice-President recognize her gift? Perhaps the display would encourage receptivity to his recommendation. Logic and the government playbook would dictate his moves. She would fall in line because that was the correct response. She was a career politician. Three generations of high standing officials. She knew the steps to this dance. They just had to go through the motions.

The Allied Planets Executive party logo disappeared. Zaambuka straightened and smiled.

A slender pale-skinned man appeared. Definitely not the Vice-President. Zaambuka stopped smiling.

"Good afternoon, I am Undersecretary General Littalik assigned to Vice-President Ramo. How can I help you, Mr. Zaambuka?" Littalik preened, running his fingers over his thinning rodent-tailed mustache and beard. His eyes did not reflect his own toothy smile.

"Put me through to Ramo," Zaambuka demanded.

"Now, Mr.—"

"Priority One, Level Seven B, Code Omega. Put me through. Now."

"Very well, Commander. Please be patient."

Infuriating. The screen flickered and Zaambuka assumed he'd been shunted back to the Senate's main operator. On closer inspection, he realized the caramel-skinned woman on his screen now was older, more poised and exuding confidence. Her blonde hair was quaffed and styled in the usual government fashion. Citriss—the Vice-President's assistant. They shared a mutual respect borne from their individual offices. It was, at last, a step closer to where he needed to be.

"Commander. If you would please wait a few more minutes, Vice-President Ramo will be with you shortly."

"Ms. Citriss, you know I retired. It's no longer Commander." She nodded, though he didn't think she would change her mode of address. "It is imperative that I speak to her."

"I understand. However, you must appreciate the Vice-President receives over thirty calls a day, all urgent, all Priority One." The woman tucked a stray strand of blonde hair behind her ear and eyed him calmly. "I've bumped you up the order. She will be with you soon."

Zaambuka twitched his suit jacket straighter and ran his fingers over his tie. "Thank you for your—"

"Citriss? Is PST still on the line? If he hasn't hung up in a huff yet, put him through."

Zaambuka's jaw tightened at the instantly recognizable voice of the Vice-President drifting through his holonet speakers.

Citriss flushed a light shade of red, but her voice remained steady. "Yes Ma'am," she replied. Raising her eyes to Zaambuka, she said, "Vice-President Ramo will see you now."

*

Their conversation had been short. Zaambuka had warned the Vice-President of the threat to her life and she had swiftly assured him it wasn't an issue. He then insisted it was a credible threat and she had cut him short.

She had *cut him short.*

Her naïve willingness to stand and face a known death threat rankled. It was undisciplined, emotional and illogical. Her response should have been predictable. Upon his warning of the threat to her life, she should have gratefully accepted the augmented protection detail and agreed to give her summit address via holonet relay. He understood the importance of the summit, but the Vice-President's life had been specifically threatened. He expected his warning to have been taken more seriously.

But no, she had refused to change her presentation to be given remotely and now he had to increase the security presence on Midock without being obvious about it and with less than a week's notice. Frustration at being dismissed burned in his belly. There were steps. Her response should have been as per the guidelines. That's *what* they were there for.

There was a gentle tap on his door. "Sir?"

He welcomed the distraction.

"Yes, Mary?"

His assistant stood by the open door. Her hesitant behavior made him itch to help with whatever drama she was overwhelmed by this time. Fortunately, it was only her nature and not her competence that was uncertain. Agent Delle insisted it was an act Mary put forth for his benefit. Delle didn't like the woman, for whatever reason, and went to great pains to irritate her whenever they were in the same room.

Mary twisted her pale fingers in front of her waist. "You have a secure line call, Sir."

"Put it through." Mary closed the door as she left, and a moment later his communication disk trilled. "Yes?"

"Zero code clearance," a deep voice barked.

Zaambuka snapped upright, the instinctive response triggered by the blast from his military past. He replaced the disk and reached for his earpiece instead. His private communicator, the one he'd been issued with as a Defender, vibrated softly. With a tap, he activated the call.

"Zero code clearance."

Zaambuka provided his old code. This many years after his resignation, it should have been deactivated, and it was, on an official level. Now, it served as a method of identification within his old team.

"Zambie?"

"Bob?" Zaambuka's eyebrows rose at the sound of the other man's voice. He and Bob had gone through Defender training together. "What are you calling me for?"

Bob had stayed active when Zaambuka got out—retired, discharged, voluntary retraction—whatever you called it. Zaambuka had been forced to leave the Defenders in order to take command of the PST—the Protection and Security Taskforce. Some of his colleagues had taken it as abandonment. Bob had understood.

"I have something big."

"Official?"

"Would I be calling you like this if it was? Zambie, it's eyes only, but high up—all the way up. I need you to handle it. An extraction, too, if you can manage it."

Zaambuka's gut clenched. He leaned forward as if he could grab his friend through the disk. "Where are you?"

"Border space. It's a bit crowded out here, buddy. Better bring your icebreaker. I'll be waiting at the old bunkhouse with the bad lighting, you remember?"

"Yes." Zaambuka flipped through his call list to check which of his agents were available. "Crowded" meant enemy forces; "icebreaker" meant a cordon blocking descent to the planet. Joy. But Bob had said border space. It didn't make sense. Sounded like something Zaambuka needed answers to. Who was after his friend? He needed superior firepower and a large team. Bob's next words stopped him cold. "Keep a lid on this, Zambie. No outside assistance, no reports. Chain of command is compromised."

Zaambuka's eyes widened. He reported direct to the President. If Bob was saying what Zaambuka thought he was saying … he couldn't trust anyone. His pulse ticked up at the thought of returning to the thick of the action. "I'm coming to get you myself."

He'd send Agent Delle to handle the Vice-President. This was more important.

*

LOCATION: Redacted

Weapon held in front of his chest, finger on the guard, Zaambuka tapped the wood of the underground safehouse door with his free hand. He stepped from view and waited. The tunnel rose only a foot above his head and, though it was steelcrete-lined, there was a damp-dirt smell clinging to the stale air around him.

A triple knock sounded back. Zaambuka waited. After counting to sixty the triple knock sounded again. Zaambuka immediately tapped twice.

The door swung inward. Zaambuka raised his gloved hand, waving it in front of the opening.

"Zambie?"

"Bob."

A hand reached through the door, grabbed a fist full of Zaambuka's thick body armor and dragged him inside. His friend was lucky he hadn't been shot. Bob grinned as if he knew it too. "You look like shenghi."

Bob's usual glowing black skin had the tight stretch of starvation. "How'd ya get through the cordon?"

"I'm a better pilot than you."

"Oh, har har. Listen, can you get us off this rock?"

"You don't want to stay? There's a rustic sort of charm to this place. Company, hunting, fishing. Ideal getaway, am I right?" He scanned the saferoom. The old flash bunker had been repurposed years ago to act as one of a series of safehouses that ran from the border worlds to the core of the Sector. It was quite homey. Rack to sleep on, cold store and even a mini library to keep the boredom at bay.

"Get away is what I want to do. Away from *here*."

"My ship is stashed. Took a few hits on entry but it's functional. You ready to vacate?" Zaambuka smirked at his old squad buddy. The grin he expected from Bob didn't come. "Bob?"

"Listen, if I don't make it out, take this." He handed Zaambuka a recording cube.

"What? Of course we're getting out of here. Keep it."

"No, listen. Rumuld is dirty."

Zaambuka's heart felt like it stopped. "What?"

"It's a recording of a meeting. He's talking to the Ascendancy."

Zaambuka's heart thumped back into a rapid beat. Rumuld. The President's brother. Meeting with the Ascendancy. It sounded insane. Rumuld was a fool. A gambler. One whose self-belief was greater than his skill. Could he be compromised? Forced into a high stakes game by a smarter foe? Xendia, no wonder Bob ordered mission silence.

The President would be on his way to Midock, where he, alongside the Vice-President, would shortly preside over the biggest peace-time vote in history. Did he know of his brother's betrayal? Agent Delle should be getting to Midock, if she hadn't arrived already, to watch over Ramo. But who was watching Marcus Hemalter?

First things first. Get Bob to a new safehouse and worry about the President's brother later. "Any patrols?"

"Not for a few hours."

"Right, so we have a window." Zaambuka took the lead and raised his weapon. "Or we're due for one. You armed?"

"Ten percent charge left."

"Here." Zaambuka bent at the waist and pulled his spare piece from his ankle holster.

"Cheers, pal."

"Stay sharp." Zaambuka flipped down his goggles and felt the confirming tap on his back. He swung into the corridor beyond the saferoom.

Light feet let them travel silently, alert to any sound, as they headed three clicks without a word spoken between them. Heart thumping a steady rhythm, his breathing slow and regular, Zaambuka realized his adrenaline spike had come as natural to him as breathing. He'd missed live action.

A double tap on his right arm slowed his steps. The corridor was pitch dark around them—not a concern given his night-vision googles. Zaambuka examined the green glow of the path ahead. At the end of the corridor was a ladder stretching up into the shadows. No heat prints. Still, Bob had stopped him for a reason … a metallic ping nearby set his pulse into preparation mode, his muscles twitching, waiting to explode into movement.

Bob crouched and slipped past Zaambuka's targeting sights. Zaambuka followed in his wake. The two men moved in concert earned through long practice, and approached the ladder steadily, constantly checking for the slightest change in their environment. A flick of red was Bob's warm fingers in Zaambuka's goggle sight. A flash and two fingers pointed up and out—split at the top. Zaambuka shook his head, whipped off a glove and gestured wildly.

The middle-finger response raised Zaambuka's lips in a smile. He pressed past Bob and scaled the ladder one-handed, the other gripped his weapon tight, holding it scant inches above his head. Before he hit the closed hatch, he locked his arm around the final ladder rung, shut his eyes and shoved his goggles up onto his forehead. He opened his eyes on the darkness, waiting for them to adjust before he moved again. The black didn't relent. Breathing deep, he crept higher until his shoulder was braced against the hatch. Slow or fast? Either way, as soon as he cracked the cover the countdown was on. Bob's hand movements below had warned Zaambuka the hatch squeaked. Best to move fast. In a burst of action, he pressed up with his shoulders and popped the lid, his head and weapon appearing first, examining the gray slender-trunked trees and undisturbed orange-red leaf matter covering the ground. No movement.

He waited for a count of thirty before he lifted the hatch higher with his arm and clambered from the hole. He knelt, placing the lid down gently and swept around in his crouch, visually casing the area, weapon primed, and listening for any unusual sound. After a moment of silence, the birdsong native to this planet returned and filled the air with tweets and trills. A crisp breeze brushed his skin. He didn't have that crawling sensation that warned him the enemy was nearby, so he relaxed infinitesimally. The distant suns, a tiny speck and a thumbnail sized ball, sat high in the violet sky. All normal.

"Clear," he muttered. Bob popped his head up, swept out of the hole and took up a position at Zaambuka's back. Neither man moved. A moment later, Bob rose to his feet. Zaambuka slipped his googles back on and adjusted them to day view, activating his tracker back to his ship. A little light blipped onto his terrain map.

He gestured to the right and creeped into the woods. No matter how slow he stepped, leaves crinkled beneath his combat boots. They'd have good warning if a patrol approached.

His mind split focus. While the forefront of his attention was on his immediate surroundings, the back of his mind returned to the implications of Bob's information. There was only one person he could contact with this information. And he had to speak to her—in person—before her speech. He'd drop Bob off on his way to Midock.

This time, Ramo *would* listen to him.

*

LOCATION: Midock * Grand Senatorial House *
Zaambuka thanked Citriss with a warm smile and entered the Vice-President's small suite, pleased to find the room fully enclosed with no outdoor access. That Ramo had come here against his advice still rankled, but she was here now. All he could do was rejig his plans to suit the active situation. Bob's news and the files on that cube were disturbing. He wasn't sure he should even tell Ramo what he'd learned. There was a possibility, however remote, that she was in on it too. Should he wait and investigate further? He figured her behavior now would inform his next course of action.

Vice-President Cat Ramo was dressed in the official robes of a ceremonial government event. It looked rather uncomfortable, pulling her posture sharply erect and limiting the movement of her head. Her black hair was tied up in an ornate twist with loose tendrils artfully escaping to caress her pale cheeks, softening the look of her outfit somewhat. Still, she'd hardly be able to move freely in the event of an attack. It was a constraint he would have to work around.

The Vice-President's angled eyebrows drew him back from his examination. Her eyes were the clearest, sharpest blue he'd ever seen, radiating with clear intelligence and more than a hint of annoyance.

"Madam Vice-President."

"Why are you here?" she asked. Determination set hard as stone on her face. Cat Ramo commanded attention and obedience. He had to convince her of the danger and insist she abort her mission. This would not be a pleasant conversation, but the guidelines were clear. A threat to the life of an official necessitated a lockdown until the perpetrator was in custody and the threat eliminated. "Where is your agent?"

"She's not here?" His thoughts darted. That could not be good. He shook off his concern. Toni could take care of herself. "I will act as your personal guard until she arrives."

"The head of the PST acting as a bodyguard? Is that not a little beneath your paygrade?"

"Are you suggesting the Vice-President of the Sector is not worth my time?"

She smiled at his win on that round and changed the subject. "How long have you been on Midock?"

"I arrived shortly after the start of the first session. I think it's going well."

The woman pressed her fingertips to her eyes, a rare exposure of weakness. "No one informed me of your arrival."

"As was my intention. As long as you remained unaware of my presence, anyone watching you would also be unaware. I've confirmed your suites are not being monitored. I believe the opportune time for an attack will come during your address."

"Suppose there is no attack?"

He bit back a sigh. So it was to be like that? How disappointing. "That is a rather childish hope to bet your life on, Madam Vice-President." He leaned forward, intent on convincing the exhausted woman of the seriousness of the situation. They had to enact the threat playbook and get the situation under control. Ramo's stare flared with anger. He could see she would fight him at every turn. At any other time, he would have relished the battle. Just not now—not with her life at stake.

The Vice-President leaned back in her seat. Her stare locked him in place. "I cannot refuse the podium on the assumption that I have been targeted for assassination. This is the most important moment in our history. Our children will look back on this day as the day the universe changed. I will not have them say it was the day I failed."

Infuriating. His gaze traveled around the small room as he thought about how to respond. The landscape on the wall depicted a natural wonder off the coast. A series of rock stacks standing sentinel over the beaches. The emerald green sky, a sunset of glorious color. "Madam Vice-President, it is no assumption. The threat is tangible. I wish you would take it seriously."

"I do take it seriously, Commander. I know what you are asking, but I refuse to cower on a *what if.*

I will not delay my speech, nor will I cancel the remainder of this summit. It is too vital. You say you are here to prevent an attempt on my life. I suggest you do just that."

"I will work to minimize the risk, Madam Vice-President, but if you take the podium, I cannot guarantee your safety."

"Then it is not guaranteed."

He forced back his anger, opening his mouth to remind her that if she were injured or killed, the vote would be annulled and her life's work would collapse in an instant, her legacy upended.

Before he could speak, she asked, "You've searched and sealed the Grand Senatorial House?"

"Yes, Madam Vice-President. We've conducted a thorough search of the building for explosives and concealed weaponry. I have been reliably informed that a new weapon is in play here, one that won't register on our scanners. It is why I am urging caution and—"

"What happened to your agent?"

He refused to be distracted. "The assassin is a shadowlink named Jase Balandez. He may have assumed the identity of a Senator on the floor or concealed himself in the building somewhere. If you are determined to speak, I must ask that you to remain alert at all times. Security will flood the floor and I will be at your side while you are at the podium."

Her eyes flashed though her voice remained soft. "Very well."

He released the breath he held. Now that he had her agreement, he could move onto the next matter. Her full focus was the summit. She wasn't compromised. It was clear she believed in the honesty of the process. "I must inform you of some information that has come to light about the President."

The moment his words registered, she sat up straighter. "What are you talking about?"

"My organization has had a certain member of the presidential party and several members of the Senate under investigation over the past year. A large sum of money was recently received into the President's family account, and subsequently moved into several accounts found to be controlled by one individual. We traced the money back through a series of political donations to a planet on the Sector One–Two border."

"That … doesn't sound too bad."

"My agent on the ground is dead. Before Gerge … he got out a transmission. A recording of Ascendancy spies in Sector One space."

"What?" She paled. "The money is from—that's not—you said the President's family account. Who received the money?"

"The President's brother."

Ramo pondered that, remaining silent for several long breaths. Zaambuka waited her out.

"Who has made this allegation?" she asked.

"A confidential informant."

"Confidential?!"

"I cannot divulge his identity, Madam Vice-President. Suffice it to say I fully trust his information. He is a credible source and it is a credible accusation."

"Of the President's brother?"

"Yes."

Ramo shook her head. Zaambuka could understand her confusion. The President's brother, Rumuld, was an idiot, but a traitor ...? "There have been several private meetings."

"That does not mean—"

"I have copies of a number of documents, Madam."

"And?"

"They are *highly* incriminating. I also have reports of other meetings and detailed discussions."

"Are you suggesting ...?"

"I am confirming, Madam Vice-President. We have evidence Rumuld has conducted several clandestine meetings with members of the Ascendancy at the order of the President."

Ramo's gaze darted around the room as she processed the implications. "The President is currently unreachable."

"I saw you gave his welcoming address. Is he unwell?"

"No idea. I need copies of these reports. I must review them at once."

"I only mention the reports to demonstrate the Ascendancy has already infiltrated this government. Do not underestimate them, Madam Vice-President. Your life is in serious danger."

"The reports, Commander."

He sighed and held out the data cube.

"You believe my murder is at the behest of the Ascendancy?"

"I do."

"I understand the seriousness of this threat, but I cannot cancel the vote. More than ever an alliance must be formed, or the Ascendancy will succeed in their pre-emptive strike."

Zaambuka stood and bowed his head. "I assure you, I will do my best to apprehend the assassin before he strikes, Madam Vice-President."

"I know you will," Ramo replied.

*

At least she accepted the offer of extra protection.

Zaambuka stalked the hall outside the Vice-President's quarters, speaking quietly into the comm-receiver pinned to his collar. He ordered an additional squad of STCT—Specialist Terrain Combat Troops—to the main hall, and a second squad to scatter along the corridors outside. No one was permitted in or out. Anyone identified as suspicious would be detained until the conclusion of the summit. He could only hope his groundwork would be enough to keep the Vice-President safe.

He paced, impatient and agitated, as he waited to escort her into the hall. He flipped the catch off his holstered weapon, his fingers brushing the grip. The attack would come soon. He could feel it. So he would remain at Ramo's side throughout the night, and he had no intention of being subtle about it.

SOOGIN

LOCATION: Space Lanes K.fleesek.657 Outside Midock Entry Point F * Battleship *Dayraider* *
Captain Soogin of the Redflag's seventh squad battleship *Dayraider* stared at the shelf that ran the length of the wall in his private quarters and pondered which of his ancient books he wanted face out. The Commodore's journal of the ten-year border war was signed by the Commodore himself, and would certainly make a statement to anyone who came inside. Or perhaps he should place his award there instead. Received two years prior for solo piloting his Sunscape through the Bwigt asteroid belt. Solid gem-cut crystal. He tried them both, standing back to view them at a distance. He exited and re-entered his office. The Commodore's book was more eye-catching, with its bright emerald cover.

"Captain." The voice came from his collar comm-receiver.

He brushed a heavily tanned finger over the microphone to activate it. "Yes?"

"You have a call, Sir. Shall I put it through?"

Soogin pursed his lips. "Who is it?"

"Dalmith, Sir."

Soogin straightened, though there was no one there to witness his maneuver. "Yes. No, wait. I'll take it on the bridge." That way his officers could bask in Soogin's presence and Soogin could show them off to their patron.

"Yes, Sir." The commsman replied. Naturally, he would not question Soogin's order. The commsman knew the men would want to display their pride in Soogin's command.

Soogin strode to the bridge. His officers snapped to attention as he entered, and he did not put them at ease. "On screen if you would, commsman."

"Aye, Sir."

The screen that had displayed their forward course through normal space turned black as it switched to holonet view. As soon as Dalmith sighted Soogin, he ordered, "Yank a ship designated *Blackflame* from forcedspace. Take the captain into your custody and await my arrival."

Soogin stared at the oversized man on the screen in astonishment. "You want me to do what?"

Dalmith, a muscular white man covered in thick swirling tattoos, glowered. His bushy black beard and eyebrows accentuated the glare. As menacing as Dalmith's usual look was, Soogin didn't think much of it.

He glanced over the bridge to gauge the attention of his crew. Seven men, women and others studiously ignored him and the man on the screen. "A ship will enter your section in three hours," Dalmith said impatiently. "Take its captain alive."

"Yes, Sir."

"It must not reach Midock. Do you understand, Soogin?"

"Of course. Midock, you say?" He projected confidence as he spoke. "Ships from all over the Sector have been through here non-stop in the last day or so. Is this something to do with the peace summit?"

"That is not your concern."

"Point taken. I will need some information on this ship and her captain. I can't stop every ship that passes through this area of space. As I said, there have been many vessels. You don't want me to stop the wrong one." Soogin winked as he spoke and ran a finger along his thin mustache, preening a little. It was joyous to be called upon to do one's duty in this way. In his head, he rubbed his hands together in glee.

"Everyone's a comedian today."

To Soogin, Dalmith's grimace looked like a grin.

Knew he liked me. All of the stories he'd heard of Dalmith snapping the necks of those who crossed him couldn't be true. After all, a man with a sense of humor wasn't all that bad. He shot another glance around the bridge. Not a single head turned in his direction. He knew they were listening and gloried in their attentiveness.

Dalmith wasn't Gallian, of course. It would have been better if Gallian himself had called. The credentials that would have loaned Soogin ... well, he already had their respect. Still, it would have done wonders for his reputation. Dalmith's good word would have to do for now.

"The ship is a '352 Jackdes Hegnforth lightship, model sixteen, designated *Blackflame*. Her captain is a woman named Delle. Toni Delle. A PST agent. You have a problem with that?"

Soogin pursed his lips. His perfect posture gave nothing of his thoughts away. Still, he allowed concern to flavor his tone. "It'll be dangerous taking an agent. She gets off an emergency message and we'll have PST agents up to our ears out here."

"Then you had better ensure she doesn't get a message out."

"Agents have unusual modifications. If she has a booster sequence or—"

"Your crew can't handle this job?"

Soogin straightened imperceptibly. "I didn't say that. Don't worry, we'll have her on board and in chains within minutes of forcedspace emergence."

"The *Capacitor* will arrive in three and a half standard hours. Have the agent transferred from your ship to the *Capacitor* as soon as you are in range."

What? Gallian's flagship is coming here? Soogin kept his face smooth, but inside he danced. "Very well."

Soogin gestured for his commsman to close the call and stood at attention for a few moments longer. *Gallian here? Glorious.* He ran his hands over his uniform and straightened the creases. Of course, there were no creases. There never were.

His gaze then traveled over his crew. Perfectly sharp uniforms. Groomed and clean cut. He was proud of every one of his people. He sniffed lightly. Only the crisp scent of recycled air and the aftertaste of space. He turned sharply on a polished heel and strode to his office.

"Captain?" The voice of his commsman stopped him before he reached the door. "Your orders?"

Soogin turned to address the man. "Contact Commander Jeophsen and instruct him to meet us at the provided coordinates in one standard. Ensure that at least one Anti-Ticyon Stream generator ship is with him." How proud Soogin was to have an ATS, one of the rare vessels capable of ripping a ship out of forcedspace, at his beck and call.

"Aye, Captain."

Soogin stood on the bridge a moment longer, surveying his command. His officers snapped to obey his orders without question. His decision to leave the APE's military to take up the seventh squad's command had initially caused him consternation, but after experiencing the professional standards of the highly paid Redflag fleet, he'd quickly lost his reservations.

In the past year, Gallian had called upon the Redflag for many jobs like this one. Soogin had yet to have visual contact with the man directly, receiving Gallian's orders through Dalmith, his second-in-command. Soogin was sure it was due to Dalmith's good favor that he received the most profitable jobs.

"Message received and acknowledged, Captain. Commander Jeophsen states they will arrive within one standard at the coordinates specified."

"Good." Soogin decided to remain on the bridge. His officers loved his close attention—they took as much pride in their work as he did. He lowered his body into his command chair and said, "Mr. Knicled, prepare the crew. Ensure all weapons and shields are functional and ready to be engaged on my order."

"Aye, aye, Sir."

Soogin settled his hands onto the armrests of his chair. Not long now. Perhaps Gallian would call him personally to reward him for his efforts? He could finally buy Charline that air-conditioned hovercar she'd been begging him for. Perhaps, he would surprise her with those space-opera tickets she wanted for her birthday too. Yes, his world was bright, and getting brighter every day.

DALMITH

LOCATION: Battleship *Capacitor*

It was a kheghing disaster. Gallian was spitting fire and Dalmith couldn't deny his involvement or throw blame onto one of his underlings.

"Your network! *'I'll have the shipments in place with plenty of time to prepare—'* Uxt was a disgraceful performance." Gallian paced. His steps were slow, even. Dalmith hid his fury, staring stoically ahead, receiving his negative performance review the only way he knew how. When he was alone, he would vent his anger in a more appropriate fashion. He had last felt this way on Carpathia, in the prison colony. Forced to accept his sentence, and helpless to do anything but watch time tick irreversibly and inevitably onward. Unable to do a thing to change his fate. Any second now, he expected a shiv in his side.

He couldn't even argue. It *had* been a monumental khegh-up. Dalmith debated blaming the agent. The clear-skinned freak who had a burning need to ruin all of his plans. Somehow, she'd discovered he was out of prison and had uncovered his plans. She'd found the guns on Uxt and those damned shippers. Just like at the Waystation. Once again, that whore's daughter was at the center of his ruination. He kept his mouth shut. Gallian didn't want excuses—he wanted results. Dalmith grit his teeth and stared at the wall, awaiting his punishment.

Gallian paced through his line of sight again. He glanced at the woman standing by the door. "Ralinna. Handle it." Gallian then stopped in front of Dalmith. His suit was pristine, his hair shiny. He wouldn't want Dalmith's blood all over him. Dalmith let his eyes focus on Gallian's face. The look in his eyes sent a spear of icy pain into Dalmith's side, worse than any shiv. Death lived in Gallian's gaze.

Dalmith nodded, accepting Ralinna had been given the role he'd kheghed up. Six months spent making his mark, impressing his presence on the thugs and crooks who worked for Gallian. Finally, they viewed him as the boss in the boss's absence, and now this? The Helkington brothers—brother—was under control. Unfortunately for Dalmith, Gallian had been forced to step in again. *Khegh it, that's it, isn't it?* Gallian was punishing Dalmith for putting his trust into a gambler who had stolen and sold on a handful of the Resonators to cover his debts.

For all the work Dalmith had done for Gallian, and for his loyalty, he should have been rewarded, but Ralinna had stolen the role right out from under him. For one damned mistake? *Khegh!* Since his early release from the prison colony at Gallian's hands, Dalmith had worked up the ranks, getting closer and closer to the man, partially to express his gratitude but mainly to regain his power. Having once run his own empire, before that kheghing agent shut him down, he knew what power bought. Control, strength, fear. He wanted that again, and by working for Gallian, he had found that once more. But he was not the boss this time. He'd learned in prison that you had to bide your time, wait for the right moment and then strike when no one was watching.

Ralinna was Gallian's go-to for private jobs. Dalmith swore that role would be his, soon.

He shuffled his feet, boots catching in the carpet pile. The *Capacitor* flew through space, stars sliding past the viewing window at the speed of a brisk walk. The boardroom they stood in ran the length of several tables. Dalmith was sure Gallian had only picked this room to flaunt his power. Typical. *Pretentious asshole.*

Ralinna—the boss's torturer—nodded, accepting her assignment. Her hair cascaded around her pouty face in a fiery sea of red, blood-tipped fingerhorns poked between the strands. Her green skin glowed beneath the boardroom pin lights. If she weren't so dangerous, she'd be a fun diversion. Dalmith smiled to himself. If she weren't so dangerous, he wouldn't be so interested.

Gallian speared Dalmith with his blazing gray stare. "You will finalize the project."

Of course. The project. A one-time event. His entire role would be to coordinate the Redflag crews. He bit back a sigh. *Khegh*. He was going to have to deal with that self-loving khegher Soogin. "I thought …" It slipped out. Gallian would have his head if he wasn't careful.

The boss's reaction was exactly as Dalmith had predicted. "What?" There was murder in those eyes.

Dalmith smiled as he seethed internally. "I'll see it done."

Gallian sipped from his black crystal tumbler and turned toward the door. Dalmith's expression slipped into a scowl. The man could have at least offered them a drink.

Ralinna followed Gallian out and shot Dalmith a slow smile as she passed. A shiver ran over Dalmith's tattooed skin. When she was out of sight, he stomped the other way, exiting from the rear of the boardroom. The project would be completed soon, and the next phase of their plans would commence. He must get back into Gallian's good books before then. He was determined to be on board Gallian's personal ship for the next phase. The trip would be a bore but the payout … the payout would be worth it.

But how? He had to do something that would impress Gallian …

The agent. That bitch who'd sent him to prison. The one who had found out about the guns on Uxt and destroyed them. Yeah, if he could get her out of the way … that would work. Gallian would like that. Dalmith scratched his beard. But how?

The agent was following the shipments. That was how Dalmith would find her. He'd send an alert to each destination receiving the weapons and put a kheghing bounty on her head.

Dalmith stopped at the next viewing window. He peered out at the starscape. The cold emptiness of space had always helped him think clearer. It was the instant death the vacuum of space promised. An equitable death, uncaring of position or how kheghing rich a person was. Just death. Even the stars symbolized death, burning themselves to nothingness.

Thinking of death, he activated his commdisk. A nervous voice answered. "Mr. Dalmith, Sir?"

"Helkington. Did the shadowlink make contact?"

"Uh …"

Dalmith's chest muscles tightened, sending a spasm of pain along his spine. "What's wrong?"

"N-nothing. It's all … there's nothing to report."

Dalmith could feel his teeth wearing away as he ground them tighter. "Explain."

"There, uh, there was a delay, but it's all sorted."

Dalmith slammed his eyes shut. His anger spiked and his fist met the wall. Pain radiated through his hand and up his arm. When he pulled his fist back from the steelcrete, he found a bloody dent left behind. He mashed his finger on the commdisk, ending the call, and snarled, stomping back down the corridor toward the ship bay where his vessel *Stalker* was docked.

More mess to clean up. Helkington would explain and it had better be good, or he wasn't going to like what happened to him next. Dalmith had to clean this up before news got back to Gallian.

"Khegh!"

*

LOCATION: Uxt – Gualliun System

It was not a good explanation.

Dalmith's fists made short work of the men in Helkington's office. Blood painted every surface by the time he'd finished. Two bodies and one unconscious idiot on the floor. He'd drag Helkington back for Gallian but, khegh it, he had to fix this. It was a fecking disaster. The agent had help. And she knew about the assassin.

Breathing hard, Dalmith straightened and his back cracked loudly. No. He *could* fix this. He'd call Soogin. The Redflag would stop the agent from reaching Midock.

Khegh! Dalmith launched Helkington's desk across the room and roared. His anger haze found the slumped body and his blood pounded hot and thick as he contemplated how easy it would be to snap the man's neck. He wrapped his hands around the skinny khegher, squeezing hard before he managed to blink back his fury. Air fired out of his nostrils as he puffed. He flicked his hands, spraying blood across the room. After a moment, he bent to latch a meaty fist around Helkington's ankle and towed him toward the door.

*

LOCATION: Battleship *Capacitor*

Soogin, that fool in the ridiculous uniform, was dead. Yes, they had the agent in their grasp at last, but two ships lost! Dalmith grit his teeth and slammed his fist into the wall of his quarters again and again. That woman, that agent. He wanted to wring her kheghing neck and see life drain from her eyes. Pain tore through his hand as the webbing between his fingers split, his previous wounds reopening.

Gallian would be pissed. Furious. And Dalmith would bear the brunt of his anger because he had called in the Redflag. He should have grabbed her himself.

Too late now.

His commdisk buzzed with the expected summons. *Khegh!*

*

Gallian stopped in front of Dalmith. "I'm disappointed." That was all he said. The blows Dalmith expected didn't come. No gun appeared in Gallian's hand.

Dalmith held the man's stare. "I'll fix it."

"You will."

Dalmith swallowed as Gallian strode to his personal ship. The hatch slid shut behind him. Dalmith stood still, silent, waiting for Gallian's ship to depart the bay, and then he let out a roar. The *Capacitor*'s energy shield was exposed by the large hull door sliding aside. A second energy shield sprang around the walkway, protecting Dalmith, the parking bay attendants and the guards from explosive decompression.

Through the observation window, he watched Gallian's personal ship zoom through the shield and disappear into forcedspace, destination classified.

"Leave the door open," he snarled toward the seated attendant. Dalmith spun away. *I should have been on that ship.* Instead, he'd have to kill the agent and take care of Midock. Given the tight timeframe, he'd have to leave immediately, but he refused to let the agent live one second longer than necessary. He should have been relieved he was still alive, instead his anger burned a hot scar in his belly at Gallian's betrayal. Dalmith should have been on that ship to meet their new partners. *I'm not trusted.*

His next growl vibrated inside his chest and got stuck in his nose. He turned to snap at the three Dober guards hovering a respectful distance away. "Take the agent and the smugglers into the cargo hold and kill them there. I want the security feed sent to my vessel."

"Sir," they replied as one. Dalmith pushed past the three men and stomped across the bay to his snub-nosed ship *Stalker*.

If he must miss the agent's blood gushing hot and sticky over his hands, he could at least replay the footage of the savage beating at a later date. To gain Gallian's favor back he would handle the Vice-President himself.

BALANDEZ

Everyone knew *of* him, but no one ever *saw* him.

The dark figure crept along the second-floor corridor, unseen by the senators, aides and PST security agents patrolling the closed area above the main hall, ducking into shadow at every voice or footstep that sounded. He possessed a definite humanoid shape, though he was not a man as rumor made him out to be.

When this assignment was over, he would blend back into the crowd and disappear. He was not a political activist, nor did he do it for money. He simply accepted death as the one constant in the universe, and aimed to cause as much of it as possible.

The shadowlink stopped outside the target door. A brief pause decoded the lock, another prepared the room inside and removed the air-conditioning screen from the wall. He oozed into the duct, replacing the screen before slithering down the chute beyond. In barely a breath, he had exited onto a small balcony high above the Senate floor. Heavy blinds covered the balcony's lip, rippling in miniscule increments at his movement.

He lowered into position near the window overlooking the Senate floor and spent several silent seconds turning the small plastic pieces he'd concealed over his body into a compact but powerful machine bow. He liked this weapon. It was easy to handle, quick to assemble, and extremely effective. He focused the crosshairs on the crowd below and scanned the seated masses until he located his target.

Happy with the sightline, angle and focus, he loaded the single projectile. He had one shot—he would only need one. The assassin cradled the weapon close to his chest and settled in to wait.

*

Time passed in a blur. Lowering the bow, the assassin focused on thinning and darkening his skin to the color of the curtain. He peered cautiously over the ledge. Vice-President Ramo was scheduled to give her speech shortly. Her final speech, though she didn't yet know it.

She would descend from her seat, walk straight to the podium and drone on about the peace treaty and the alliance and cajole her audience to vote her way, unaware of his presence above and the modified weapon aimed right between her two hearts.

This was the moment he lived for. The rush of excitement that flooded his veins, the pound of blood in his ears, the entire room narrowing until only he and his victim existed. A dance of life and death. An intimate breath between him and his target. He had a need to see their life fade from their eyes, to know he had taken that light and extinguished it between his own fingers. Each death was a treasured memory. The first. His father. As indeed every shadowlink must. A life for a life, as tradition states. But he had not stopped there. The taste of sprayed blood on his tongue, the sticky sensation between his fingers demanded more. A thirst that could not be slaked. Each kill became cleaner—the thrill greater. His mother's light. His master after that. He learned to stalk, to slip into the shadows, to take his time. The sovereign! Yes, they had been a delight to take. The mistress of Zir Helpma—the holonet star—livestreamed to her horrified fans. An exquisite moment in time.

This one. This death would outshine them all.

He sighed, the air barely puffing his lips. Tension tightened his body. Taking a moment to savor the delicious feeling, he returned his gaze to the crowd.

The politicians fell silent as the Vice-President rose. The assassin smiled broadly and settled in to listen. The moment had to be just right. She would give it to him. His fingers stretched around the bow.

Without intention, he zoned in on the drone of the woman's voice but, as she made her sudden and startling accusation, he shifted up and into position. He raised the loaded weapon and pressed forward, his heart increasing the speed of its beat even as his body froze.

The room below grew quiet. He didn't hear it. He was mesmerized by the woman in his sights. His stare fell to her neck and the flutter of her pulse. With the slowest of movements he drew the sight down until the crosshairs centered on her chest.

Taking a deep breath, he released air slowly through his dry lips and, at the point where air no longer existed, he pulled the trigger.

TIKE

"Hey Tike, caller for ya. It's the angry dude. He wants to talk. Says it's important. I told him ya didn't want to be disturbed, but he won't go away."

Tike pulled the damp towel from his face and scowled. "Ahhh, khegh it. All right, put him through." His second-in-command, Mikko, had called Tike via the audio-only speaker imbedded in his wrist wrap. Tike swiped at the water on his chest and shoulders and tied the damp towel around his waist.

"Thanks, man. He sure is an ugly dude, ain't he? There ya go, have fun."

The tall Tyrazoid shook his elongated head, spraying water droplets around the room. His green-grey pores soaked in the rest. He grabbed his commtablet from his clothes pile as a face appeared. Mikko was right, of course. Dalmith was butt-ugly. Bald with a black beard, the giant man was covered head to foot in tatts. His eyes were small and black, and his nose had clearly been smashed in a time or two.

"Are you prepared? The timing must be exact."

Oh, it was just a nervous ney-ney check-in. The dude needed to calm his shiz. Tike had it handled. It was a matter of respect. "Don't worry about it, big guy, it's under control."

Dalmith grunted at the insult. "You've received the shipment?"

"Yeah, we did, and about time too. Four days late. My boys thought you were having us on, but they've examined the weapons now and they're anxious to try them. You said they're powerful. Don't look it. Could pass as regular laser rifles."

He had thought about taking one out and playing with it, but Dalmith's orders had been clear. His money had been even clearer.

"Be sure that no one—"

Again with this? "I said it's under control. We've got a large screen set up in the base, connected to dozens more scattered over the planet. The minute that pretty Vice-President buys it, we'll start the party."

"You must be sure to kill the King during the first few minutes of the riot."

"Yeah, yeah. I know." Tike straightened his shoulders. "Hey, Dalmith, the gangs on Endeavor Seven and Hjimen Twelve said their shipments were different. Is that right? What's going on?"

"That is none of your concern."

Inwardly, Tike sighed. Mikko had it right. The dude was angry. He fairly vibrated with it. Tike ran a hand through his damp hair. Distance from the man made him cocky. "Well, I reckon it is my concern, isn't it? As I hear it, we're part of something bigger. My boys and I want a larger cut."

"You will receive what you earn. Your team will be given first choice of future work ... if you complete the job. Do not expect more or I will take our business, our weapons and our money elsewhere."

No need to get prissy. Tike didn't say it. He couldn't afford to lose the coin this job would bring him and his lads. The rep he would build with this job would mean he and his boys would finally be top gang around here. They'd control the streets, and with the King dead, his royal security forces would be forced to withdraw and regroup to protect the palace. The streets would belong to Tike. "I get it, you don't have to spell it out. Was checking up on me the only reason you called?"

"Isn't it enough?"

"Point. We'll be ready for the signal. I swear that on the King's blood."

"Better swear by your own."

"Yeah, right." Tike went to break the connection, but the screen turned dark before he could hit the button. Dalmith always cut him off first. *Khegher.*

Tike dressed and stomped from the bathroom. Mikko hovered just outside—a muscular vision of manhood. Pity he didn't shower more often.

"Well, Boss?"

"Wasn't important." Tike snagged a beer bottle from the fridge. Dealing with Dalmith always left a bad taste in his mouth.

The eating area was as basic as it got for an operation like this. A cooler, utensil tub and a basin. As far as Tike was concerned, you spent your coin on bathroom facilities before anything else. The warehouse was just wall panels and a smooth crete floor. And the weapon crates, of course. Plenty of those. Mikko's men were hooking up the holoscreen. Tike could hear 'em cursing up a storm. Going well then. The rest were tossing dice around the makeshift Chariji table and cheering raucously.

His gaze drifted to the stacks of crates. *Khegh Dalmith.*

"Mik, what say you and me grab one of those new guns and test it out topside?" he suggested as Mikko came up beside him at the cooler.

"Thought you said we weren't supposed to open the crates."

"What's Dalmith gonna do to stop us? I wanna get a feel for the damage it does. Need to plan, ay? How close we need to let the boys get to each target."

"Sounds fair." Mikko smiled, exposing sharp eye teeth.

Tike sculled the bottle and dropped the empty into his second's outstretched hand. He grinned. "I've even got a target in mind. Bezo's workshop."

"Nice, Boss. That khegher's had it coming for snitching on Ferek last year."

Oh yeah, that royalist khegher would get what was coming to him, as would the man he swore his loyalty to. No more decrees. No more land stolen. No more kidnappings off the street never to be seen again. No more exorbitant taxes no one could ever hope to pay.

Tike grinned.

The King wouldn't see it coming.

*

The guns were like a dream. Bezo's workshop had dissolved—as had Bezo himself. The boys were excited for the games to get underway.

The tension in Tike's body ramped up as the Vice-President on the screen—a stunner in a white dress—froze. For a moment, no one in the Grand Senatorial House moved. The talking heads—channel presenters—gasped as pandemonium seemed to hit the Senate floor. The Vice-President was pulled to the ground by some suited security guy and all that could be heard was screaming and shouting, including those of the talking heads, demanding to know what was happening.

Tike looked around at his men. "Something's gone wr—"

The warehouse windows exploded in a roar of noise and shattered glass. Pods spewing thick white smoke appeared as men in black suits and masks swung inside, landing between Tike and his men. The palace procession continued on down the outside street as Tike dove behind the closest crate, his weapon primed, spraying laser fire seconds later. Bloody royalist hit squad! *How did they find out?*

A thick-bodied man in a red coat and agent's silver star strode across the floor, unfazed by the laser fire tracking toward him. Not the King's men at all. These were core soldiers. And a bloody agent was leading them! Tike's men huddled around the Chariji table and beneath the holonet viewscreen. Tike glanced up at the screen. The shaking video playing showed the Vice-President crouched behind a lectern.

Tike yanked his gaze away from the screen, landing on the bearded agent. The STCT officers screamed for Tike's men to drop their weapons.

The agent approached and Tike had a whole second where he actually contemplated dying in a blaze of fire and taking the agent out with him. The moment passed.

"United Agent's Association. Drop your weapon and put your hands on your head!"

Tike raised his hands.

The sound of glass shattering on the floor above indicated the STCT had stormed the upper floors. Within seconds, Tike's entire gang was surrounded. Mikko barked out an order and the men dropped the Resonators, opening fire with their personal pieces. Tike was surprised the men remembered not to fire the Resonators in an enclosed space before pistol fire rained down around them. His men were quickly cut down and the gunfire ceased. Tike was the only one left standing. Squatting. Whatever. His gut cramped at the blank look in Mikko's frozen stare. *Khegh*. The fury welling in his blood petered out at the surrounding guns.

"Drop your weapon," the agent said with a smirk.

Tike could rage, spitting revenge for his men, his loyal boys, but it would only get him killed. And dead was not what he wanted to be. Seeing no alternative, Tike did as ordered and placed his piece on the ground. Someone had sold them out. Must have. But who?

The agent roughly pinned Tike's arms behind his back. "I'm Agent Rac Tee with the Protection and

Security Taskforce, and you are under arrest for the illegal possession of a class-four weapon. What you say to me now will be recorded and used in a jospitj court of law. You have the right to a defense. If you do not have one, then you'd better get one quick, pal, cause the ones we supply ain't all that good at getting guys like you off."

One STCT officer turned the holoscreen off. Tee's speech ended and he addressed the STCT officer at his side. "Lock 'im up."

The officer pushed Tike against the wall. Tee stepped closer to the senior STCT officer. "How did the others go?"

"Tom and Pic just called in. They report all went down smoothly. They've taken the Southern gangs without a struggle. Sheez and Ray also report success. The King is safe here. All the Resonators have been confiscated on the Northern continent. Terry Jalden on Marn just called to advise that his teams are having trouble with the gangs there. He requests immediate backup."

Khegh it all. They'd taken out Dalmith's network. That would infuriate him. He'd be looking for someone to blame.

"Send a message to Sheez and Pic, tell 'em to get their butts to Marn," Tee replied.

Tike and his men had failed. Not only was the King still breathing, but now Tike would have

Dalmith on his ass. The man's temper and fists were legendary in the darker circles. Then again, the agent clearly knew what was going on, so maybe Dalmith would go down too. One could only hope. If not, Tike was gonna die, either here or in prison. It was only a matter of when and where.

The agent approached Tike's side. "Hear that, pal? Your underworld is down. All the little riots you planned to take over the streets ain't gonna happen. Now, tell me who hired you and where you got these weapons from, and maybe we'll go a little easier on you and your boys." He looked around at the bodies. "Well, on you."

Tike remained silent. He was no snitch.

"Okay, you don't want to talk to me? We'll just haul you back to the holding cells in Carillingtrex City on Sector One Central for a little chat. You and me, we'll get to know each other real well over the next few days, pal. Come on." The agent pushed Tike toward the door.

I probably shoulda let him kill me.

CAT RAMO

LOCATION: Sector One Central * Government Palace *
The flashing light on Cat Ramo's tablet reminded her of
the time. She glanced over her outfit to ensure everything
lay correctly and she had not inadvertently stained her
shirt, then checked her small mirror. Her makeup was
still flawless. She checked the rest of the room. Her desk
was clean, though perhaps she should have asked Citriss
to remove the pile of department tablets stacked neatly
on the end. All was as it should be.

Except she was already so far behind this morning,
and had yet to finalize her speech for the summit.
Prince Chrismatt's message had caused too much of a
distraction. She flicked her microphone on. "Citriss?
Is PST still on the line? If he hasn't hung up in a huff
yet, put him through."

She grimaced as Citriss's frantic pop-up messages informed her that the Commander had overheard her ill-mannered comment. Her eyes drifted closed and she huffed out a breath. *"How completely unprofessional."* Her mother's voice was crisp in Cat's mind, her disappointment thick. *"Cat, you must never relax your political game face."* She pushed the embarrassment aside, though heat in her skin persisted.

Honestly, the time she spent on etiquette and poise felt overwhelmingly excessive, yet days like today reminded her just how important it was to remember her position. She was Vice-President. Her every waking moment was spent in awareness of that fact. The dignity of her position necessitated she push through the pain of her inappropriate behavior. She could not allow her personal grievances to get the better of her. The Prince's message must be put to the back of her mind while she dealt with her current agenda. No matter how her ego smarted at her inability to express her true feelings, she wasn't permitted a personal view. As Vice-President, her opinions were those of her office. She had grown up in public life. Politics was in her family's blood, and she truly loved her job. It was just that sometimes she had a bad day. Today was one of those days.

She breathed out and re-centered her mind using her favorite holographic image on the wall opposite her desk. A swathe of warm color—a sunrise over the

Zabni desert of her homeworld. It always worked to calm her thoughts. *"Focus, Cat."*

Her private screen activated, and she stared at the head of her government's security agencies. Antonio Zaambuka was a warmly tan-skinned man only a few years older than herself yet seemed ageless. Maybe it was his mysterious gray eyes.

The head of the PST looked agitated, going by the deep lines around his mouth. Her unprofessional comment probably hadn't helped his mood. Or perhaps that was not entirely her fault. She eyed the garishly multi-colored tie he wore in the old human-style. *"Good Xendia, why would he choose to wear that monstrosity?"*

"Vice-President Ramo. I appreciate your time." He lowered his head in respect to her position, but his eyes blazed with a contained fire he barely managed to keep from his fine modulated tones.

The smooth behavior tickled her embarrassed ego and sharpened her response. "I must say that I am displeased with your treatment of my staff." *"Really, Cat? Attacking him? Hardly dignified. He's doing his job, and besides, you were the one to disrespect him first."* Oh, there went her mother again. "I apologize, Commander. I have had a difficult morning, though it is no excuse for my poor behavior." She pushed her frustrations further into the background of her mind. The Commander had done nothing to warrant her anger.

She released her breath slowly and schooled her facial expressions into that befitting a woman in her position.

"It is no longer Commander, Madam Vice-President, as you well know." He blinked. "Please call me Antonio."

"Too personal, Sir. Surely you know better than that?" She cleared her throat. "Mr. Zaambuka, what is it you wished to discuss?" She blinked but the colors of his tie had burned into her retinas. "Excuse me for saying this, but where did you get that awful tie?"

The lines between his eyebrows deepened. "Just Antonio please, and you sent it."

"Me? I assure you, Mr. Zaambuka, I have better taste than that."

"And yet I received it from your office." The muscles around his eyes twitched. "Vice-President Ramo. My call is to ask you to withdraw from the Midock Summit."

For a moment, all breath left her body. She could feel her mouth gaping. *"A terrible loss of self-control."* She pulled herself together, her anger spiking. "You are joking?"

"I am not. I have been advised of a credible threat in regard to the summit. There is no need for your physical attendance. I suggest that you give your presentation via holonet relay."

"What?" Had he not bothered to do his homework before he called? She ground her teeth together and pain flared in her jaw. Her gaze flew up to her homeworld holoimage again before returning to her screen. "Mr. Zaambuka, the summit is being held at *my* behest. For you to suggest I not attend is a ludicrous proposition."

"Then I must insist one of my agents join your protection detail as your personal bodyguard. I will provide additional security teams to monitor and assess the safety plans and vet the attendees and their associates on a deeper level than currently required. We may need to consider limiting access to the facility on the days leading up to the summit." His smile didn't go anywhere close to his eyes. She could feel the steel in his words through the screen. Well, if she was doing her job right, he would feel hers too.

"You will not."

"Vice-President Ramo—"

"I will not have you jeopardize this project. Any dramatic increase in security will convince the representatives of the Confederacy that we are not confident in our ability to keep our own people safe. It will tell them we suspect trouble. This is not a message I intend to send. This is a time of trust and cooperation."

Zaambuka blinked and she had a feeling more bad news was coming. "Madam Vice-President, I have strong reason to believe your life is in danger. The threat is tangible."

He truly had no understanding of the delicate nature of her work. "I am sure you are correct. However that cannot be allowed to stop me. Fear of a possibility cannot stop hope. Peace can be achieved. We must manage the risks."

"Madam Vice-President, your life is not a risk to be taken. Do you honestly believe your undersecretary can continue on in the event of your death?"

He was looking for her to flinch. He didn't know her. She would not. This was *her* meeting. *Her* time. No one would take it from her. How dare he use the Undersecretary against her. Everyone knew Littalik didn't have a subtle bone in his body. "Of course."

"You hesitated, Madam Vice-President. Why?" Zaambuka lowered his voice, leaning infinitesimally closer. "My agents have uncovered evidence indicating there will be an assassination attempt. I am recommending the President—out of an abundance of caution—give his opening address via holonet relay as well. Now, my teams will arrive—"

"No."

"Vice-President Ramo!"

"Listen to me, Mr. Zaambuka, We must be on location. It is imperative that we greet our guests in person. I will not have squads of security officers on top of my own security staff, the President's teams, Senate protection *and* the Confederacy's security officers.

There will be plenty of security at the meeting; if anything too many—"

"Double them."

Damn him. That was her own inner voice. "Mr. Zaambuka, I will consent to your top agent. If he is as good as you say, there should be no further trouble. However,"—she spoke over his objections—"I will accept a *slight* increase in the number of patrols and have *one* officer added to each door. That is as far as it goes. We must maintain an atmosphere of trust. The summit will be streamed live via the holonet. We must be transparent. I will not have you calling all of our hard work into question."

His eyes flared. "Madam Vice-President. Your life is more important than—"

She cut him off. "Enough. You know exactly how important this is. We will never have this opportunity again. Sector One and Sector Two in one room together? *Nothing* is more important."

He took a visibly calming breath. She had him now. "Yes, Madam Vice-President."

"Mr. Zaambuka," she said, and cut the connection.

How dare he speak to me like that? Cat squeezed her eyes shut and stood. Anger drummed inside her chest and she could feel the veins in her head pulsing. The door opened and Citriss stepped inside.

"Inform security there will be some changes." Cat's voice was full of venom. Citriss was the only one she could be herself with, but even Cat could hear how infuriated she sounded and didn't want her assistant to think any of her bad mood was aimed her way. Cat pressed her hands to her belly, closing her eyes as she breathed out.

How dare Commander 'call me Antonio' Zaambuka undermine her like this? She'd spent *years* preparing, suffering through endless meetings and pouring on the charm. She'd suppressed her feelings and conducted painstaking leg work, supplicated and sucked up to incompetent government officials, only to have it all brought down at the last hurdle? No. She would not allow it. She would turn this to her advantage. There *must* be a way.

"Cat?"

"Citriss, I need a moment, please."

Extra agents were more acceptable to her than stepping down from this moment in history. The project had been delayed far too many times over the years, and if it were put off again, she seriously doubted it would ever take place.

She heard the door close with a soft click and opened her eyes. A headache spray and glass of water had been left on her desk. Cat sprayed once up each nostril and sipped at the water to rid her throat of the bitter aftertaste. There had to be a way to spin this. She just had to find the right lever.

*

LOCATION: Midock * Grand Senatorial House *
Cat didn't know where the week had gone but here she was at last, preparing to speak at the most momentous moment in history. A peace summit for the ages. Her greatest triumph. Yet still the barriers were rising against her. Cat leaned forward in her seat and locked eyes with her assistant. "Citriss, I need you to send an urgent message." They were bunkered down inside her temporary office in the Grand Senatorial House on Midock, the room change her concession to the threat on her life. She'd requested the move to an internal office—a tiny one—with no windows and only one way in and out. It was all rather claustrophobic.

Citriss tried to bite back a grin that Cat saw clear as day. "Of course, Madam Vice-President."

"Citriss!"

"Sorry, Boss, but you know I have to be formal here. If the Undersecretary walks in to find us gossiping ... well, we are *supposed* to be hard at work." Citriss brandished her glass dramatically, now happily refilled to the brim.

"We *are* hard at work." Cat argued. Thank heavens for her friend. This entire week had been a tense wire, taut to the brink of snapping. Citriss always knew when Cat needed to relax. Hence the lockdown and libations.

Citriss leaned back into the deep sofa and cradled her glass to her chest, "What's the message, Boss? Who am I sending it to?"

"Antonio Zaambuka, Commander-in-chief of the Protection and Security Taskforce."

"Oh, I don't think I'm going to like this. Why do I always have to send these messages?"

"Because I'm the Vice-President and you're my assistant." Cat sipped from her own glass, resting her head against the back of the giant armchair. At Citriss's sudden gesture, she pulled herself straight, not wanting to destroy the elaborate hair-do so painstakingly created hours earlier. Within days, she would know if her hard work had been successful. "What am I going to do with myself this weekend?" Cat mused.

Her friend huffed and drained her glass.

"My entire life has been building to this one moment. Years of work, sweat and tears. You know Mother sent me a message this morning to congratulate me? She just assumes we will see success today."

"She's very proud of you for following in her footsteps."

"She has very large boots, Citriss," Cat snorted. "How do you measure up to the woman who consolidated all of Sector One's underperforming, ineffectual and disparate planetary administrations into one reasonably functional government?"

"If you achieve this, Cat, there will be no comparison."

Cat rose from her chair and paced the floor of the tiny office, placing her empty glass on the desk as she passed. The train of her official Vice-Presidential dress was held gently between her fingertips. If she ever became President, the gaudy full-length trains of the traditional outfits would be the first thing to go. Events such as this summit were ceremony heavy, but the lengths of the weighty robes were simply ridiculous. Oh well, it was something to put on her *to do* list. After the success of this summit—and it would be successful, she refused to accept otherwise—she could turn her focus to the election. The President's behavior over the last few weeks, well months really, left a lot to be desired. The people deserved better. She could give it to them.

Upon their arrival at the Grand Senatorial House, the two women had retreated to Cat's office to await the official commencement ceremony. The opening had been delayed by the last-minute cancellation of the President and the late arrival of the Confederacy's representatives.

And hadn't that call from the President's office been a bit of fun?

"What do you mean, he's not coming? He is scheduled to give the opening address!" The most important day on the political calendar for this decade,

and the President was not coming? Had Commander Zaambuka succeeded in his scare campaign? Was Marcus fearful of his safety?

"I'm sorry, Madam Vice-President. I don't know what to tell you. He gave me the order only moments ago. The President will not be in attendance. He expresses his apologies, and asks that you fill in."

"Fill in? The representatives from the Confederacy are here to vote on an alliance between our two Sectors of space, a decision fraught with massive political and economic ramifications, and he wants me to fill in? I have my own address to contend with, and he wants me acting in his stead? It's my summit. He'll usurp my success. Acting as him will give his office full accolades no matter what I achieve here."

The President's personal assistant winced but covered her lapse quickly. Her flushed face told Cat she was genuinely embarrassed by her boss's behavior.

It was simply unacceptable.

"It is a great honor, Madam Vice-President."

"He's going with that, is he?"

The woman sighed, "Honestly, Cat, I don't understand either, but he was extremely insistent."

Yes. Insistent that he not do a thing. His behavior, while disappointing, was at least consistent. *A great honor, my butt!* Cat suspected the senators out on the floor were already restless and anxious for the proceedings to get underway. Add in the time to symbolically open the summit—a speech she would now have to hastily write—with their impatience and the uncomfortable outfits … The government officials would be on the knife's edge of a bad mood. It was not an auspicious beginning.

"So, what do you want me to tell him? The Commander?"

Oh yes. Her message to the Commander. Ex-Commander. He certainly gave off a military vibe regardless of his now civilian position. "Inform Mr. Zaambuka that his squad of *troopers*," Cat stressed the word as heavily as she could, "arrived hours ago, but his *top* agent hasn't shown up yet. Tell him I cannot stall for much longer. If his agent is not here in another half hour, I will be forced to give the opening address without his protection."

"He won't accept that."

Cat glared unhappily at the blank tablet on her desk. *How can Marcus let me down like this? Oh, be honest, Cat. You're more annoyed because you actually expected him to turn up and didn't have a speech already prepared to give in his place.* "We'd better get to work."

*

"And do the representatives of the …"

The Speaker's voice washed over Cat in a gentle hum. As her gaze traveled the crowded room, she gloried in the culmination of all her hard work. It appeared every chair in the grand hall had been filled. The Grand Senatorial House, built when world membership of the APE had grown too large to fit comfortably into the Senate chambers on Ctalnez Seven, was based around the Mixitt horseshoe principle. The senators from the thirty-five original member races sat at a large semi-circular table in the center of the hall, and the sixty-five newer APE members sat behind them on a raised circular platform.

Cat was at the left of the semi-circular table. It put her on the lower floor, closest to the dais. Peering around at the men, women and others talking softly, she wondered which way they would vote. The long-eared Maybeez were culturally isolationist, the people from Telber and the colorfully skinned Shantels, dressed in their usual drab grays, were both popular and gregarious. In contrast, the gray-skinned men from Cig'malae, seated directly opposite Cat at the other end of the table, dressed somewhat gaudily in their traditional robes of greens, reds and fluorescent yellows, tended to favor a wait-and-see stance.

The room was buzzing with anticipation and a growing impatience for the speeches to begin. Senator Kalzee'tiam sat to her right, midway between Cat and the Cig'malae representatives. He peered down his long white nose at the crowd of onlookers, aides and assistants seated behind the member states and shook his head. He seemed to sense Cat's attention and sneered over at her. His frame was similar to the Undersecretary's, though his skin a lighter shade. She stared him down, refusing to be intimidated. Ugh, ever since their schooling together Kalzee'tiam had insisted upon this petty rivalry. So what if she'd beaten him in every school political debate? That was school. This was peoples' lives. He needed to grow the hell up. Eventually, he turned away, leaning down to listen to one of his assistants, and the tense moment was broken.

Cat's gaze continued around the room. Someone here planned her assassination. The uneasy feeling in her skin only grew stronger the longer she remained still. Someone, somewhere in this room was willing to see her die today. Who could do that? And why? Her gaze shifted back to 'Tiam. He would not miss her. Though he would not be so blunt about it. His lackeys and followers, however, might not have the same reservations.

At the open end of the lower table was the newly installed dais. The podium on the dais had been miked to ensure the orator could be heard throughout the hall. When Cat glanced toward the rear, she could see the area reserved for the holomedia behind a large transparent barrier. It did nothing to mute their noise—she could hear them demanding to speak to their individual planetary representatives before the speeches got underway.

Today, the hall overflowed with members of both the APE and the Confederacy's parliaments, and it was positively seething with excitement, rather like a live beast, sides quivering as its breathing quickened, anticipating fight or flight.

Cat's opening address had gone well enough. As stressful as it was, they all knew why they were here. She welcomed the representatives of the Confederacy and spoke of the intention of the summit, calling for honor, respect and adherence to the law. Ultimately, the beings in this room, representatives of hundreds of worlds, would vote to decide if the APE and the Confederacy should join forces in a political conglomerate. The successful result meaning peace and cooperation for centuries to come. *My legacy.*

Across the floor and seated on the circular platform level, the Confederacy's representatives talked quietly amongst themselves. If they were anxious at all, they hid it well. Prince Chrismatt of Jaalex sat regally in the middle of his advisors on the second level opposite Cat's position at the table, a single point of calm in an ocean of chaos. The handsome black-skinned man stared steadily around the room until his eyes locked onto Cat. She felt a jolt of awareness travel down her spine. *Whoa.* When the Prince returned his attention to the Chairman, Cat felt released and sagged back in her seat. Well, that was unexpected. And not at all unwelcome.

Undersecretary General Charly Littalik, seated beside Cat, caught the look and leaned close to speak into her ear, "Prince Chrismatt may be royalty, Vice-President, but he was elected into his presidentship fairly. It has been over a hundred years since a member of the Jaalexian royal family has held a position of power."

"I've read the reports," she replied, leaning slightly away from the cloying presence. Littalik, a whip-thin man with a long beard and tailed mustache, had a tendency to press too close to whoever he spoke with. His white skin was shiny with sweat. "Nevertheless, the Prince wants this alliance as deeply as we do, and he has the celebrity to make it happen."

"Of course, Vice-President," Littalik agreed. "With the rise of the Ascendancy, it does not surprise anyone that the Confederacy wish to align with a government as powerful as ours—one that is firmly dedicated to peace. I merely hope they don't intend to hide behind the APE's skirts and rely on us to save their asses."

"That's enough!" Cat glared at him sharply before returning her gaze to the Senate floor.

It was her hope to sway the abstaining senators to her cause rather than fight to change the minds of those firmly fixed in their decision. Senators Patral and Jezba from Telber would vote for the alliance. Senator Sahz'bi and Senator Tr'Dik were Kalzee'tiam's staunchest supporters and traditionalists—they would vote against. Senators Ke, Ral and Soochik of the Cig'malae would wait until they heard both sides of the argument before they stated their intention. As for the senators who remained, Cat had no idea which side they favored, though she had her suspicions. They would be her primary focus. She must convince them to join her cause and vote for the alliance.

The fear of imminent Ascendancy attack would bring out the best and worst in her fellow politicians, and all sides would be seen here today. Cat had to be better. She had to believe. Her cause was just, and the truth would win out.

*

Time passed and not a lot happened. She shifted, crossing and re-crossing her legs uncomfortably. Twenty-eight hours of sitting made the soft, imported ciplec-wood chair—the wood that molded to one's body—feel like a steelcrete board. Her back ached, and she was finding it increasingly difficult to concentrate. The constant disruptions and eruptions of obnoxious name-calling and heated words by the usually mild-mannered senators had exhausted them all.

Cat worried the purpose of the summit was being lost beneath all the petty squabbles.

Proceedings paused as Prince Chrismatt walked to the podium.

He held a quiet, commanding presence in the face of the Senate's obvious hostility. He expressed his appreciation for the chance to speak and his deep voice carried over the agitated room, instantly hushing the crowd. Cat's pulse thrummed faster. *Please let it go well.* She had viewed many previous addresses made by the leader of the Confederacy and knew him by reputation as an honorable and charismatic man. If only they had been able to speak before the official proceedings began. She hoped he would speak well of her and her intentions. All this hinged on his favorable acceptance.

The Prince's gaze rose to the high ceiling of the hall, arching over them like a giant wave, and traveled to the balconies on the second and third floors. Cat followed his gaze. It was a truly beautiful room, and the perfect place to confirm a lasting treaty of peace. She hoped he thought so too. He spoke softly but his voice was full of steelcrete.

"We are here today to vote on the alignment of the Allied Planets Executive Party and the United Planets Confederacy against a common enemy. A remorseless enemy. A bloodthirsty enemy. An enemy determined to enslave, decimate, and destroy.

"As many of you know, my homeworld is located close to the border of Ascendancy space. I have witnessed neighboring worlds lost to the Ascendancy's encroaching armies. I have comforted families who have lost loved ones to the ships that advance across our borders. I have held my own grandmother through her gut-wrenching sobs when we were notified of my brother's death at Ascendancy hands."

The emotion in Chrismatt's voice brought Cat near to tears. Knowing how closely she was observed, she blinked them back. It would not do to show too much emotion. 'Tiam's cronies would only see it as a weakness to be exploited. She held back from glancing over at the man in question. She would give him no hint as to her thoughts. 'Tiam was a shark in a pool full of sharks. Her every move, flinch or smile would be torn apart by the man for the slightest advantage.

"The Ascendancy has strength in numbers, a well-trained battle force, and an unquenchable desire to rule. They will not stop, they will not hesitate, and they will not retreat. When we are gone, who will stop them?" Chrismatt paused, closing his eyes. He breathed deeply. Cat was touched by the raw honesty in his expression. "Only together can we fight this unrelenting encroachment on our territories. Only together can we defeat these twisted, dark souls working to pit us against one another. Do not wait until they have destroyed us before you decide to act."

Oh, please let the wavering senators hear the truth in his words. She pressed her sweaty hands to her skirts and hoped she wouldn't leave prints behind. If

Chrismatt's impassioned words did not stir their audience, how could Cat ever hope to do so?

"I have the support of my government and of my people to make this offer here today. Align with us against the Ascendancy. Stand with us, side by side, and say *no more.*" He eyed each senator at the table and those gathered on the level above. After a moment, he shifted his gaze to stare directly at Cat. She felt his presence fill her soul. It was as if he addressed only her. "I support an alliance between us. I thank the spirits of Trelner, who protect us in this time of uncertainty, and I pray they guide us here today to make the right decision."

She offered a smile. He tilted his head and returned it. As he stepped from the podium, the room exploded in a cacophony of voices.

Hope stirred in Cat's chest.

The Prince acknowledged the congratulatory remarks offered as he passed each senator and, once seated, looked to Cat again. She felt mesmerized, as if he spoke inside her mind. *"Up to you now."* The pressure was immense. Her hands grew damp again.

"Wow, look at that response."

Cat tore her gaze from the Prince to glance at the man beside her. "Yes, we have cause for hope."

The media, stacked three deep at the back of the Senate hall, screamed question after question and were only placated at the promise of personal interviews with their planetary officials at the next break in proceedings.

It was almost half a standard before the Speaker of the House restored order. For the first time that evening, Cat took the delay as a good sign.

*

Senator Kalzee'tiam approached the podium, his every movement an expression of his arrogance and righteous outrage. His thin frame loaned him a tall visage, increasing the perception that he looked down on them all. Cat suppressed a groan. *Here we go.* 'Tiam leaned over the podium and glared at Prince Chrismatt, hissing loudly, "Do not be fooled by the Confederate Prince's exaggerated sense of morality and his play to your emotions. What threat, I ask you? Sector Three has every right to enforce the protection of their own borders. Are we suggesting each Sector no longer has the right to defend their own people?"

From the Princc's cohort arosc a loud cry of protest. *Oh, of course.* Cat breathed through her nose to keep her expression in check. She had hoped for intelligent debate. She should have known better.

Kalzee'tiam ignored the protest and lifted a hand high in the air. "Praying to long dead gods for assistance—is he serious? We have not been attacked.

There is no evidence of Ascendancy armies waiting for Sector Two to fall so they can attack us. Prince Chrismatt is asking us to send *our* soldiers to *their* borders to fight an army whose only goal is to strengthen and protect their own lines against the Confederate conspiracy.

"And make no mistake, if we were to send our troops to aid the Confederacy's imaginary battle, we will weaken our own defenses, freeing the Confederacy to launch an attack on *our* border. Join with them, he pleads! What a subtle way of saying, 'We want access to APE troops from within.' This cannot be borne, this *will not* be borne!"

The rumble in the room grew louder. Cat could make out angry whispers and catcalls amongst the crowd. 'Tiam was stirring up old hatreds and reinforcing traditionalist views of sovereign borders. It would be a mighty battle to sway those so set in their beliefs. Negativity swelled, forming black shadows around the worst of the naysayers.

All Cat could see were furious faces, sneers and bitter snarls of teeth, seething bodies made horrific in her imagination. It had to be one of 'Tiam's traditionalist supporters who plotted her murder. Only an extreme event would completely derail this day. Perhaps she should have heeded Zaambuka's words ... but no, they would not do it here, not live on the holonet feeds. No, that would give her all the power.

Zaambuka's warning would not prove true. She hoped it was only nerves and not fear that dried her mouth and swept her heart rate into orbit.

Am I being naïve? 'Tiam would glory in her failure. If he didn't achieve it via conventional means, would he be so emboldened to commit such a horrendous act himself? No. If there was to be an attack, it would occur after the vote. She was betting her life on it.

"If the Ascendancy attack Sector Two, then I say let them. It is not *our* fight. Let both sides weaken themselves, and when their war is over, they will have no desire to take us on. In the meantime, let us strengthen our own borders and build up our defenses," one senator cried. All Cat could see of him was teeth and sharp nails.

"The President is not even here today. Is that not the clearest indication we have that he does not support his own Vice-President in this matter?" another shouted.

Ugh. She'd known 'Tiam and his support circle would take advantage of that.

Kalzee'tiam smiled, acknowledging the point. "I challenge Vice-President Ramo to make public what evidence she has that proves the Ascendancy intend to attack," he jeered and pounded his fist against the podium. "I demand she show us the declaration of war. I demand an immediate dismissal of this so-called vote until such evidence is received and re-viewed!"

If only it were that easy. Cat knew the evidence was plentiful but those that did not want to hear the truth would never hear it. She held her composure when 'Tiam glared at her. She would not give him the satisfaction of reacting to his words. His sneer implied he knew he'd gotten to her anyway. How could she fight his fear mongering without sounding hysterical herself?

'Tiam swept imperiously from the podium and sat down. The room erupted again, this time in fury, with accusations shouted from every corner of the hall. Cat could hear one question repeated constantly, "Where is the President?"

She wondered that herself. Marcus had supported the alliance—had always given Cat his full support. Of course, his non-attendance here spoke of a need for a way out. If Cat failed, Marcus could imply he'd never truly supported her or the alliance. Did he know something she did not?

The Speaker called for a break.

Cat stood to stretch her legs. As she rose, fatigue settled heavily across her shoulders. What she truly wished for was to slip back to her office for a quick nap, but as the recess was announced, her advisors moved in, demanding she alter her speech to include a response to both Prince Chrismatt's and Senator Kalzee'tiam's arguments.

At the time of planning the agenda, she'd thought speaking last would give her the best chance to appeal to the entire room. It meant that now she must overcome every negative thought and supplant it with one of hope and trust. An impossible task. She just didn't have time to sway the undecided.

Her advisors were at pains to remind her that every senator present, and the citizens watching the live holonet feeds, were relying on her to make *the* speech to sway the vote toward peace. At this point, Cat feared her best would not be good enough.

As tired as she was, she took the time to review her advisors' arguments and, on their suggestion, did alter some of her speech. As the doors to her private suite closed, Cat sighed and leaned against the desk. In the time that remained before they reconvened, she wanted a moment to herself.

Before Cat could even remove her shoes, there came a knock and Citriss opened the door. She mouthed an apology as she escorted Antonio Zaambuka into the room.

*

The head of the PST's arrival heralded a truth that was completely unpalatable. Marcus knew of his brother Rumuld's involvement with the Ascendancy. He had to. And it explained his absence. What she couldn't reconcile was his motive. Did he stay quiet because he didn't want his association to interfere with the vote or ... or was he truly against the alliance? By Xendia herself, was Marcus ... a traitor? It was too much to process. Her brain felt saturated with the new information. She couldn't comprehend the news.

For good or ill, her meeting with Zaambuka had worked to settle her nerves. His information about Rumuld drove all fear for her safety out of her mind. But how could she sway the senators to vote her way when she was beginning to doubt the integrity of the process herself? The files: holograph images, planetary civilian closed-circuit video and numerous audio recordings provided by Zaambuka were damning and, in her mind, conclusive. She had no doubt Rumuld had done as accused.

She glanced at her notes but inside her chest was a chasm of pain. *Betrayed.* If Rumuld had the support of his brother, then regardless of the vote's outcome, he could hand Sector One to the Ascendancy on a platter. If the vote succeeded here today, she would condemn Sector Two as well. *I should stop this!*

"What's wrong?" Zaambuka hissed at her as they walked down the corridor.

Surprisingly, his presence was a comfort. It was her mind and emotions that were in turmoil. "I ... I can't ..."

He spun back and pressed close to her side, his voice sharp. "Do you still believe in the alliance?"

Did she? Remove Rumuld and Marcus for a moment, did she believe in a peaceful alliance? By oath, she did. "Of course." And that had led her here, standing before the combined political hopes of two-thirds of the galaxy. No pressure.

"Then be brilliant. Focus on that."

"How can I—"

"Because you are Cat Ramo. You do your job, Madam Vice-President. I will do mine."

Cat shielded her eyes from the lights flashing rapidly at the back of the hall. The holonet media were going crazy, pressing forward against the temporary barrier that barely held them contained. If only they knew. For a moment, the magnitude of her task froze her solid. It was her duty to convince these representatives that every vote mattered. Each and every one had the power to change history, and somewhere, here in this hall, someone was waiting to kill her. *The President's brother is a traitor.* What was she supposed to do? Her blood thudded inside her body—too slowly, like drel-honey—and her brain was only working at half speed, but she knew what she had to do. *Tell the truth.*

Breathing deeply, she blocked fear of judgment, of being found wanting, of failure, and focused only on her breath as she exhaled. She imagined air stretching from her mouth, floating out over the crowd, expanding until it filled the entire room and returned to her more powerful than ever before. She opened her eyes. So many faces stared back at her. Hungry, desperate, murderous. For an instant, fear gripped her again, closing her throat and freezing her lungs.

I can run. It wouldn't take much. If she ducked through the door at the side of the stage and slipped her handlers, she would be on her own. She could disappear.

The urge passed and she breathed deeply once more. She wouldn't run. She had chosen this life and this path. She would not fall apart now.

The white noise of chatter dulled and the hall fell silent.

At her shoulder, Antonio Zaambuka was focused on the crowd, his hand resting on the weapon at his waist. He caught her look and their eyes locked. The corner of his lips twitched in an *I'm glad it's you and not me* smile before he tilted his head. *Go on.*

Silence sat heavy upon the majestic hall, stifling even the tiniest sound associated with shuffling limbs and shifting bodies. Cat imagined her voice ringing out like a bell across the room, her skin faintly green, luminescent beneath the spotlight on the dais. A lone star in a pitch-black sky.

"Every concern raised here must be respected and honored. Today, I will address your arguments and hope that when the time comes, your decision will be made with an informed mind and confidence in your choice." Cat endeavored to make eye contact with every senator she could, noting who gave the appearance of listening and those who flat out refused to meet her gaze.

Focus. The speech is all that matters. Kalzee'tiam had highlighted the APE's lack of evidence against the Ascendancy to undermine the urgency for an alliance—a clever ploy. If an attack was not imminent, then there was no need to ally with the Confederacy right now. Several speeches today had urged caution and to approach the alliance with steady yet conservative forward steps. She had to convince those senators that an alliance now would benefit both Sectors. Not just as a partner against a common enemy, but as a partner with mutual economic and financial benefits. Growth, stimulus, travel, infrastructure. There was so much to be gained from this one decision. This moment was bigger than her. Bigger than her ego, bigger than her legacy. *This is for the people.*

For the first time, Cat let go of her desires. This was not about her. It was about them. It was always about them. The people. The future.

Cat's voice traveled confidently to every ear. "This is a unique opportunity, one we will not see again in this generation, perhaps in any generation. A chance to change the life of every being living in our two Sectors today.

"The economic and financial benefits that come with aligning with the Confederacy, a Sector as strong as our own, are unparalleled. A Sector whose strengths lie in their comprehensive health services and strong governmental support systems. It is our mission, it *must* be our mission, to protect the systems, planets, and governments under our care, but also our people. We can do that together. As we did over three hundred years ago when the first human transports entered our Sector. We were not afraid of an alliance then, and we should not be afraid now. Humans fleeing their own world's destruction, a violent aggressive people and a people with their own culture and traditions, and we did not turn them away. Now, humans are some of the most productive members of the APE and a valued voice on the Senate. We have another chance to strengthen our borders and enrich our discoveries." She should never have made this about power or position or control. Leadership. True leadership was about the lives of her people, of support, of empathy and trust. Cat's pulse beat slow and steady, telling her she was right with her approach. Her hands were dry, her mind clear. *Hear me, please.*

"Sector Three is ruled by a dictatorship, not content to remain safely behind their own borders. The

Ascendancy's desire to expand and dominate means every world and every life is in danger of falling to their bloodlust."

She softened her voice. *Hear me, please.* The alternatives if she failed did not bear thinking about. She imagined the faces of the children, lost and alone. Of families destroyed, and lives ended prematurely. Homes, planets torn apart. The stakes were the highest they had ever been. Failing now would mean the end of everything that mattered. "We, the APE, have a duty to protect our worlds and our children. The Confederacy has a duty to protect *their* worlds and *their* children. Together, our goals are the same—to save every individual from a life of slavery at the hands of an enemy who will stop at nothing to destroy us."

Cat took a deep breath. Her optimism fading as she examined the somber faces staring back at her. If only they would listen with an open mind.

"I understand, and respect, the points raised by Senators Corini and Vlashma, and in particular that of Senator Kalzee'tiam. But I ask you, how can we, as governments entrusted with the protection of the people, elected to serve the people, afford to sit back and wait for the Ascendancy to attack?

"Signing a treaty of peace with the United Planets Confederacy is not a declaration of war against the Ascendancy, as some in this room would have you believe, but just what it is—a declaration of peace, the offer of an alliance with a people and a government very much like our own." *Please hear me.* She clasped her hands together. *The time is now. Do it for yourselves.*

"We share a common goal, and that goal can be strengthened by each other's support. The lessons of both Sectors will serve to benefit all peoples, and will create a vast pool of experience from which we can draw upon to combat the inequities facing both of our societies, and not, as Senator Kalzee'tiam would have you believe, each other."

She stared down at her speech notes, weighing the consequences of what she was about to say against the fallout of not speaking at all. If she chose to say nothing, and the vote continued unchallenged, the alliance could still be voted down. If the information came out afterwards, the resultant public horror would destroy everything she had attained. If it were then discovered she knew and chose to remain quiet …

Cat had no option. She had to speak the truth. To do nothing would make her as bad as Kalzee'tiam, Rumuld and Marcus, and that could not be borne. *Mother forgive me.* If the vote failed, perhaps one day, the process could be renewed. She prayed today would not go down in history as the day the war began. Her gaze drifted to Zaambuka and then rose to Prince Chrismatt. *Forgive me, please.*

"But how can we align ourselves with another Sector and another government, when our own leaders operate from a private and secretive agenda? Today I was informed of some very distressing news. One of our own people, a senator in this very room, has betrayed us to the very enemy we are discussing here today. Despite my instinct to deny the accusation, I was provided with proof."

Zaambuka's stare snapped from the crowd to Cat as the room erupted in a sheer wall of noise. She couldn't look his way. Her inflammatory remarks had just provided the perfect opportunity for an assassin to strike her down before she could betray them all. Security officers seeded throughout the room ran forward, attempting to reach the dais before the surging senators could reach her. Now that she had begun, she had to finish before she could be stopped.

At first, she had to shout to be heard, but quickly dropped her volume back as the room fell silent, everyone anxious to hear what her accusations entailed.

"Through a lengthy and confidential investigation, it has been discovered members of this very Senate have been dealing with parties working against our interests." The noise rose again and the room heaved. For a moment, Cat felt true fear. Everything that made her strong wavered under the onslaught of panic. *I'm throwing everything away.* Truth would win out. She would ensure it. Cat cleared her throat and spoke from the heart.

"For individual wealth to be considered so advantageous that these conspirators would consider their actions above reproach is simply beyond my scope of comprehension. These deals have been made to prevent an alliance being formed. Without an alliance, the probability that the APE or the Confederacy alone can defend against an attack is hampered, if not made impossible. By undermining this peace process, they ensure the Ascendancy will win against us all." Cat found Kalzee'tiam in the crowd and held his poisonous stare.

"If this is not a pre-emptive strike by the Ascendancy, I do not know what is. Surely, this is the evidence you have called for, evidence that demonstrates the Ascendancy is conspiring with our own people to force our submission. We must act now. We must act to prevent war."

Kalzee'tiam rose to his feet with the surge of the crowd. He stared at her with such loathing that Cat took an involuntary step backward. She tore her gaze away and peered up at the Prince. He remained seated while those around him jumped up and down hysterically. His face was troubled, but he did not look angry. She took that as a good sign.

'Tiam bellowed hate-filled rhetoric at the crowd. Not a single person paid him attention. The audience of senators and aides raged, the mood ugly and growing more livid with every moment. Cat had lost control of the room.

Zaambuka stood in front of her now, tugging her toward the protected corridor off the main hall. His other hand gripped his weapon tightly. He hadn't raised it yet, but she could see the white pressure marks on his fingers that indicated he was seconds away from doing so. Standing this close to him, she could hear voices screaming in his earpiece, ordering him to get her off the dais.

Cat yanked her arm from his grasp. She had to see this through. If she had destroyed any chance for an alliance between the APE and the Confederacy, then she must protect the integrity of what remained of her government, and that of the Confederacy, by denouncing the traitors publicly. It would be her only chance to head off the conspiracy theories that would destabilize her government for years to come.

Raising her hands, she motioned for silence. Quicker than she thought possible, the room calmed. Zaambuka tried once more to pull her from the podium, but she turned on him with a growl. He gave a heartfelt sigh and backed away, barely a step from her side and took to holding his weapon in his hand.

When she held every breath of attention in the room, she spoke again. "There's no defining mark—" The podium rocked violently beneath her hands. Her panicked gaze focused on a tiny dart imbedded in the clear microphone stand just inches from her chest.

Those seated on the front bench screamed as they realized what had almost happened. Cat stood frozen, staring at the deadly object in horror. Zaambuka grabbed her shoulder and pulled her down behind the podium. "Vice-President, we have to get you out of here." Cat barely heard him above the crowd's roar and shook her head. Her hands were like ice. She couldn't feel her legs.

The podium had saved her life but if Zaambuka tried to move her, they would open themselves up to attack. Screaming and shouting filled the air with impossible noise. There was no way off the dais without exposing them to more risk. "Where did it come from?" she whispered.

The dart angled downward. Zaambuka's head rose as he stared at the balconies lining the walls. Cat had been assured the second floor was rigorously patrolled. No one should be up there.

On the closest balcony, two figures wrestled over a weapon. Zaambuka started to stand.

"No!" Cat pulled him to the ground next to her. "Are you crazy?"

"You're a sitting daybuck out here," he yelled, wrenching his arm from her grip. "I have to get you out of here!"

"How? As soon as I stand—"

"My agent will subdue the assassin."

"And if she can't?" Cat demanded.

"Then she's not as good as I thought. Have there been any more darts?"

"No."

"That gun fires one shot. Toni will take care of the assassin before he can change weapons." Zaambuka peered over the podium and across the Senate floor. Cat creeped closer to see what he was looking at. The hall was in uproar. PST agents plus her own security were attempting to seal the room while senators and aides tried desperately to vacate the hall. Prince Chrismatt was buried beneath his security team. *Good.* Now Cat had to get out. Zaambuka had been right. She should have held her address via the holonet.

She followed his gaze as he peered up at the balcony again, but all she saw was a waving curtain. The media pushed frantically at the security cordon around the stage. How on Marn had they got so close? Their faces were alight with hunger, scenting the story of the century. One broke out, a big black-bearded fellow making his way through the crowd toward the dais. *Great time to push for an interview!*

A flash in the corner of her eye brought her gaze up again. Zaambuka's agent stood at the balcony's lip, staring down into the crush. Her hand hung oddly at her side and, even from this distance, Cat could see blood on the woman's ghost-like face.

The head of the PST rose to his full height and helped Cat to stand. "I am uninjured," she confirmed. A shout snapped her gaze to the black-bearded journalist. Her eyes widened and she screamed.

Zaambuka reacted a fraction too slow. The journalist vaulted onto the stage, leaping high above the closest ring of security, a palm-sized pistol appearing in his left hand. Zaambuka pushed Cat back and the shot penetrated his chest. He fell to his knees, his pistol lax in his now useless hand.

Cat stood unprotected as the journalist raised his weapon. He bared his teeth in glee. The sound of two shots echoed through the hall. Cat waited for pain to slam into her, waited to fall. Instead, a blossom of red seeped from the shooter's chest. He fell to the stage floor, stone dead.

Zaambuka fell back and closed his eyes. His breathing stuttered. "Oh no you don't," Cat shouted. She knelt beside her savior and ripped a piece of her skirt apart to create a bandage.

Zaambuka nodded in the direction of the balcony and Cat turned to see the woman there nod in return, grin wickedly and disappear behind the curtain.

"I guess she is as good as you thought." Cat's voice quivered, her fingers shaking as she pressed the makeshift bandage hard to his shoulder.

ZACH

LOCATION: *Blackflame* * Inside Battleship *Capacitor* * Zach woke, or to be accurate, the CII experienced a sudden return to awareness after his reboot. Everything returned with a snap. He activated his cameras and checked his systems, finding a blank spot in his memory files. *That's not good.* Running diagnostics, he located the deletion of several files. His camera footage was also fritzing.

Zach ran a second diagnostic, and played back the last few moments of his recorded memory before the … *flash wipe? Oh, there you go, plasma cannon.* Zach confirmed his visual feeds were optimal and scanned the ship for enemy souls. They were clear of brigands. Mate—the C-bot—was in the cockpit, but there was no heat signature or visual of the boss anywhere on board. Zach's vocal program was scrambled. He reloaded the drivers and rebooted his speakers. A micro-second after they came online, he attempted to speak. "M-m-mate?"

The canine robot lifted his head, ocular cameras focusing on Zach's overheads. He didn't speak. His fake fur appeared singed.

Zach tried again, "M-m-ate, what-t-t hap-p-pened?" Zach pinged Mate's connection. His remote access was corrupted—no wonder he couldn't make contact. Mate rose. The C-bot's stumble as he regained his footing worried Zach. Plasma cannons could do a lot of damage if they triggered a surge within a contained electronic system.

The C-bot shuffled into his hub and connected via his hard-line. Mate uploaded footage and memory files that he had made since the boss got him partially active. She had chosen not to repair the C-bot's vocals in order to get his access memory functioning. Part of Zach giggled in glee, or at least the CII equivalent. Mate couldn't speak.

Do not think it. The C-bot submitted directly into Zach's processor.

Zach sent back, *Buzzkill.* Checking his external feeds, Zach discovered the *Blackflame* was docked on a ship designated *Capacitor.* There was no sign of the boss.

Captured, was Mate's response.

Ya think? Zach would have to help the boss first before he could repair his scrambled code.

He sent out a crypto-burst on his remote signaler. The bursts had to be micro-seconds short to avoid detection by the *Capacitor*'s security software.

Tracking the boss was going to take a while.

*

Eventually, someone on the *Capacitor*'s bridge selected the *new menu* link Zach had texted out under the guise of advertising a staff lunch and installed his virus. With access to the *Capacitor*'s systems, Zach was able to run a search for the missing agent.

"Yup, she's in a cell," he confirmed.

Mate's vocal systems were still undergoing repair. He remained physically linked to Zach in order to communicate. *Has she devised a plan?*

Zach reviewed the last few hours of footage. *Oh, no.* The boss's interrogation had lasted over four standard hours. She did not look optimal as she was dragged back to her cell.

Mate reviewed the footage silently. He expressed a doubt the boss had given a concrete escape plan much thought.

Zach agreed. He was working to infiltrate as many of the *Capacitor*'s systems as he could, focusing primarily on external shield access and internal doors.

When the time came, the boss would need those deactivated as quickly as possible. Then a strange line of code in one of the communication logs distracted him so much he actually expressed the question via his speakers. "What is this?"

What did you find?

"A line of text has been added to the comm code—someone has tapped a secure line offship. Short bursts—data, maybe?"

Can you get more information?

"Yes. Wow, isn't that interesting? The coding is awesome."

What did you find?

Zach, what did you find?

Zach?

*

Zach had always considered himself the digital equivalent of suave, but it had taken all of his electronic charisma to convince the unknown coder to assist.

He'd hacked the file with the strange code and reached out to the author. He was forced through an elaborate dance to prove who he was without giving away where he was located. The communications were kept short.

My assistance must remain confidential.

Confirmed, Zach replied. The unknown coder typed agonizingly slowly.

You cannot tell the agent.

Zach hesitated. Not tell the boss? How could he keep this from her?

Zach?

Confirmed. Zach didn't like it, but to get the coder's help, he'd agree to anything.

I have limited access.

I need the door codes.

Easy done. The main exit out of the prison corridor will be the tough one.

How so?

Must be entered on the pad manually. Cannot do remotely.

Let me handle that.

How will you—

The boss has bad eyes.

I don't know what that means.

Doesn't matter, the boss will. Zach returned. *Can you get offship?*

I have a way.

Do it. When the boss gets out, it won't happen quietly.

A dialogue box popped up requesting access to his database. Zach danced a giddy digital jig when a password file was saved into his systems. *Thank you.*

The coder jumped off.

"Well?" Mate asked. Aloud. He'd managed to re-pair his speakers then.

"I have it," Zach confirmed.

"So, now what?"

Zach was silent for a moment. "Working on it." He had to figure out a way to communicate with the imprisoned agent and then organize an escape plan. He also had to keep their helper a secret. The boss would not be happy with that, so he'd have to make sure she never found out. Piece of pie.

DANIEL COLTEN

LOCATION: Forcedspace

From a different perspective, the two lightships appeared engaged in a strange, exotic dance. They dodged and weaved in intricate patterns, twirling and spinning around each other in graceful, long loops. Surrounded by gaseous clouds and glowing light, bright flashes jumped from one ship to the next creating a highly spectacular visual show.

Only on closer inspection could you see the gas was not natural. It sprayed from the damaged ships in fits and bursts, and the brightly colored light show, so beautiful from a distance, was laser fire spewing from both ships, hitting each other with computer-generated accuracy.

The heavily damaged larger ship spun in uneven, jagged circles. The smaller vessel vented gas more regularly and lost speed. It was unclear if these problems gave the bigger ship an advantage—the old star-roller gave the distinct impression of limping.

The smaller ship, a Stargazer designated *Renegade,* took another hit in the rear where the ship's NSD—Normal Space Drive—was located. The *Renegade*'s captain, Daniel Colten, felt the hit against his already weakened shields and rolled his shuddering ship in a tight one-eighty. He brought the *Renegade*'s rounded bow up behind the larger vessel, which—unable to maneuver as tightly—was caught broadside.

"Time to end this," Dan announced.

"Target locked," his CII, D'ena, confirmed.

Dan studied the shield status and spun his chair to face the forward screen again. "Fire!"

Through the computer-generated viewer, the star-roller attempted to abort its turn. The *Renegade*'s captain anticipated this and positioned his ship to take advantage.

The star-roller presented her defenseless side for only a moment, and in that moment, two torpedoes shot out from below the *Renegade*'s viewscreen and streaked toward their prey. Dan allowed himself the few seconds before the torpedoes hit to enjoy the timing that he'd had the *Renegade*'s Toroidal Matter torpedo bay installed at his last docking. The *Renegade* was now just as powerful, if not more so, than the star-roller lying dead in space before him.

He imagined the torpedoes hitting the star-roller, picturing the electrical current inside each torpedo flare as the magnetic field separating the materials mixed and exploded. The *Renegade* had a limited supply of torpedoes, but at this point, he had the advantage. It might be enough to get him out of the encounter alive.

The torpedoes exploded against the star-roller's unstable shields, weakening them further.

"Fire three, four, and five, two seconds apart!" he shouted, pulling the stick to drag his ship *up* in an effort to dodge the powerful lasers targeting him from the damaged star-roller's underside.

"Firing three, four, and five. Two seconds apart," D'ena's sultry voice replied.

The first torpedo erupted against the star-roller's shield, which fluctuated as the second torpedo exploded. The shield dropped just as the third made contact, freezing the star-roller mid-turn as the torpedo exploded. The rest of the ship followed in a larger, more intense explosion.

The blast's ripple wave rocked the *Renegade* wildly before Dan compensated. Eventually, they steadied, and he shut the howling systems down before they died on their own. This area of space was fairly desolate. He shouldn't be caught unawares by another ship, so figured he had time to inspect the damage before they jumped again. "Do you think he was alone?"

"No other ship has jumped in, right?" he checked.

"Question is, were they sent after us or was that just happenstance?"

"Rycee wants me dead. The result is the same." He bent to examine one of the many flashing panels around the cockpit. Tapping a well-manicured black finger against the numbers displayed, he groaned.

"How bad is it?"

He glanced up at D'ena's digitalized image. "Sweetheart, you don't want to know."

"If you don't tell me, I'll find out my … Oh, no." She groaned in a realistic imitation of her Captain's a moment earlier.

"Told you." Dan moved out of the cockpit, scooping up a box of tools on his way to the engine room. The *Renegade*, his first true love, was leaking smoke, and the scent was burning his nostrils. He pulled a large panel from the floor and bent over the open space to examine the damage. "Looks like we've lost our—" he broke off as a billow of black smoke coughed from the hole. "Shenghi!" He ordered D'ena to activate the internal fire-extinguishing system. Gray foam sprayed into the cavity.

"Hey, hey, D'ena, it's out!" he cried a minute later, sitting back on his haunches. The CII flushed the life-saving foam from the cavity and Dan ducked his head into the access tunnel to gauge the extent of the damage.

"Looks like we've lost long-range scanners. Shield three is weak, but stable, and the Cerenkov generator is offline," D'ena reported.

"Great." Dan scrubbed a hand through sweaty cords of thick black hair. He yanked it back from his face and snapped the elastic tie from his wrist over the tangled mass to get it out of his way. "Let's start with the shield." He grabbed his toolbox and disappeared into the engine room.

It seemed like only a moment later his CII interrupted his repairs. "Captain, I have located an unread message in my storage banks, and it's coded. It's old."

"What?" came the muffled reply.

"Old coded message."

Dan stuck his head up through the access hatch. "Message?"

"Coded. Old code, too. I am not sure how long it's been there or why I have only located it now. Perhaps the damage is more extensive than we thought." D'ena's digitalized face appeared on the screen to his right as Dan pulled himself out of the hatch.

"Well, decode it, sweetheart."

D'ena disappeared. The blank screen was replaced with static.

"Can't you clean that up?"

"Give me a second."

A woman's face with skin so transparent he could see the veins throbbing in her forehead appeared. Her glossy white hair was tied back from her face, stretching the skin at her temples. Dan rocked back on his heels. He never thought he'd see that face again. The woman wet her lips and the sight sent waves of longing through his body.

"Dan … Daniel. Um … Danny." The woman sounded drunk. "The Reef on Uxt. It's my place. Consider it a no-go zone for your betraying stinking ass."

"What the khegh?" Dan's mind raced. *Why call me?* "What's the date stamp on this?

"Unclear."

She'd called and he'd never received the message. "Why call me?"

"Sounds like a warning, Boss."

"Hmmm." He stared at the wall as his thoughts bounced madly around his head.

"What are you thinking?"

"What? Uh, nothing."

"You're not thinking of going to The Reef, are you? That message could be years old. She won't be there."

"Oh no, yeah. Of course."

He flashed back to the last time he saw her. That same face staring at him, twisted in horror. It was a face he still saw in his nightmares, filled with shock and betrayal. He could finally make amends. If she didn't shoot him on sight. "Boss. Rycee is still after you. Wasn't that the whole reason you stayed away from her?"

How could he explain when he couldn't put it into words? It felt like this was a sign. The attack by Rycee's top dog and now Toni's message. He couldn't pass this up. "I thought keeping her out of this would keep her safe. It did. It does, but ... I'll deal with Rycee. Don't give me that look, I will. This is a chance I didn't think I'd get."

"You're projecting."

He growled. "Watch it."

Dan glanced back at the face frozen on the screen and felt a tingle against his neck, a memory of her finger stroking his nape—warm from sleep, slow and gentle. He rubbed at skin there, only realizing he'd done it after he pulled his hand away. He sighed softly.

"I didn't think she'd ever talk to you again," D'ena said, her face appearing on the smaller screen below the main one that still contained the frozen image of Toni. Toni Delle. The PST agent who'd tried to arrest him. The agent he'd betrayed. The agent who now hated his guts with a fiery and fully justifiable passion. Xendia, this was a blast from his past that hit like the mallet of a crete-masher.

"Technically, she didn't. But why did she call?" he muttered. "It has to mean something. De, is the generator back online?"

"It is now."

"Set a course for Uxt."

"Boss."

"I know, I know. She won't be there. But ..."

"Course plotted."

"Start the link," he ordered, moving swiftly back to the cockpit.

"Link attained." D'ena's face followed him through the ship from screen to screen and stopped at the display next to the pilot's chair.

The readouts looked okay. Dan held his breath and pressed the controls to activate the generator. When nothing exploded or even sparked, he released the breath in a whuff and flicked the Ticyon Flux Field generation sequence. "If she doesn't shoot me, it might mean she'll hear me out. I can finally explain," he uttered, only partly to the CII.

Outside the ship, an almost invisible field encircled the *Renegade*. It flexed imperceptibly, the fluctuations increasing until the Stargazer shot forward and disappeared into forcedspace.

*

LOCATION: Uxt – Gualliun System * The Reef *
The first thing Dan noticed as he stepped into The Reef was that Jeri still tended the bar. The large guy waved as he spotted Dan. Three arms. Dan had heard the barkeep lost the other. He'd also heard what had happened to the shooter. A reminder not to cross Jeri—ever.

It was heaving inside the bar, and loud. Dan allowed the hinged door to swing shut behind him and scanned the room, keeping his right hand near his pistol ready to draw. This place didn't keep the kind of clientele it was wise to be weapon-less around. *Is this stupid?* It was not as though she would be here. The Reef had become a criminal hangout over the past few months, even Jasmine, the Cross's assistant, avoided the place now, and she used to love the joint. Dan just couldn't shake the feeling that this was one of those important times in your life you didn't let slip past if you could avoid it.

Dan sidestepped an oblivious waiter and sauntered toward the rear where the lighting was low, and the booths were located. He tripped, barely catching himself from crashing headfirst into a nearby table. A long leg encased in a very high-heeled boot drew his gaze up the tightly wrapped body to the masses of long red hair that didn't hide the fingerhorns poking out from her forehead. Sweaty, shiny green skin gleamed beneath the bar's fluros. As he watched, the woman examined him just as thoroughly. She raised her eyes and motioned toward the empty seat at her table. The tingle in his skin told him to check the rest of the bar first, but temptation won out. *What's one drink?*

Dan sat down and smiled at the enticing woman. She sipped her flaming Jashari and leaned forward, enough so that Dan struggled to keep his gaze on her face. His lips twitched as she inquired how long he planned to stay on Uxt.

"Who knows?" he replied.

She raised her glass. "Maybe I can motivate you to stay a little longer."

Dan stared hard at those luscious lips as she took a sip of the steaming liquid. Her tongue darted out to catch any stray drops foolish enough to escape her mouth. Feeling eyes burning into his back he shot the Nymph a flirty smile, leaned over to finish her drink and stood up. "Excuse me, won't you?" He pushed to his feet and what he saw when he turned stunned him to silence.

She is *here.*

"Don't be long," the Nymph said. Dan barely heard her. As he pushed past, the Nymph held out a hand to stop him. He looked down, and the Nymph pressed a room key across the table. Dan pocketed it with a smile, though his attention was firmly fixed on the agent sitting in the rear booth glaring daggers at him.

There's decent odds she won't shoot me in a crowded bar.

He grinned and sauntered in Toni's direction.

*

LOCATION: Uxt – Gualliun System * Lower Underground Locker Bay Nineteen*

She hadn't shot him.

It was a start.

He glanced at the locker key in his hand and his thoughts drifted back to the agent. Toni was exactly as he remembered. Feisty as hell, and their quick banter sent him right back to that moon they'd been stranded on together, like no time at all had passed. She'd hidden any surprise at seeing him, hiding as she always did behind those damned shades. And lounging in that chair had not hidden her right hand, which had hovered over her pistol the entire time they'd spoken. He was still shocked she'd asked for *his* help. She made no reference to their last time together and had not asked why he'd left her behind. It was like their past had never happened.

He peered around the endless locker bay and bit back a sigh. Lockers of every conceivable size covered every conceivable space—stacked ground to ceiling and arranged in rows that created narrow walkways between the towering columns. Stepladders and hover-pads were scattered throughout the area for the use of any unfortunate patron assigned an upper locker. For security purposes, the bay was brightly lit. Though that hadn't deterred the local artists. Graffiti created wide landscapes of color in the otherwise plainly painted bay.

Dan nodded to the guard standing beside one of the columns. It was the fourth he'd encountered in as many minutes. Lot of security here for a bunch of lockers.

Irritation itched at the back of his neck and without thinking, he scratched at the skin angrily. Toni had told him that above the bar, just outside the theme park entrance, was a locker bay for visitors to store their personal items. She needed a locker emptied. He really should have said no but he was desperate for a chance to make amends. Retrieving the contents would mean she'd have to see him again. And this time, he'd make damn sure he didn't chicken out of owning up to his ... error in judgment.

Shenghi, you shot her, you ass!

Okay, he had. And if he was Toni, he wouldn't forgive that. Regardless, helping her—for no perceivable personal gain—had to get her attention. She might listen. He had to try.

The tag on the key read 6749. Two columns to go. Dan glanced over his shoulder. *Still there.* Two men had been locked to his contrail from the moment he strode into the bay. While Dan relished a good fight, one started here would attract too much attention, particularly from those Ghil guards. With their thick necks and massive shoulders, they would tear him apart with their bare hands. He usually made a point of not picking fights with guys more than twice his size. The two humans he could handle. Two men and a couple of Ghil might be pushing his luck.

Counting as he walked, Dan reached the correct wall, crouched and fingered the door of locker 6749.

A twist of the key opened the door. Over it, he watched his tails step into view. One stopped at the top of the corridor, the other walked slowly down the aisle toward him.

Dan threw the locker's contents into a bag, secured the door and headed in the opposite direction. His tail quickly followed. As soon as Dan turned the corner, he ran.

And skidded to a halt. *Damn!* More goons. Over his shoulder, the first two moved closer. *Double damn.* He debated drawing his own pistol and decided against it. He would appear more innocent to security without a gun in his hand.

Dan plunged down the first gap in the locker corridor he found. A locker at head height exploded. He yanked his head aside—*khegh*—and ran faster, ducking low and hoping the next blast would miss. A bolt hit the ground near his heel, spraying chipped stone over the floor.

Dashing around another corner, he spied the lower-east theme park entrance in the distance and two Ghil guarding the doorway. A private entry for the park's more exclusive patrons. Past the doormen, the hall opened up onto a large glittering staircase extending from the lower ground to what looked like the very top of the complex. The polished steps appeared to be made of the same coral the entire complex was built from. Each step brightly colored, glaringly so, enough for Dan to get lost in the noise.

He skidded to a stop and sauntered toward the doormen, doing his best to steady his breathing, and holding up the card he'd swiped earlier. He knew the private invitation would be needed at some point. "Good evening, the seas are calm tonight, aren't they?"

"Good evening, Sir." The Ghil on the right replied and opened the glass door for Dan to enter.

As the door closed behind him, Dan took off through the great hall heading straight for the staircase. Above his head, high, high above, the skylights—or really the ocean light—showed that the complex was submerged deep in the sea. An occasional brightly scaled fish darted past, drawing Dan's eye. Tearing his gaze from the distraction, he stared up the glass-covered coral stairs. The staircase was packed with park and casino patrons all loudly marveling at the colors and commenting on the sensation of walking on the coral itself. Dodging the slower walkers, Dan raced up the staircase's widely spaced risers, running two steps at a time. He risked a glance back over his shoulder and almost lost his balance as the ground stretched away beneath his feet.

Two-thirds of the way up, his calves screamed to stop or at least slow down. He stared over the brightly dancing patterns of the steps and spied three more goons waiting for him at the top. "Damn."

A familiar fragrance tickled his nose, a scent he'd not smelled in years. Dan searched the crowd for the perfume's source and spotted an old friend standing at the golden balustrade a few steps above. He grinned. "Carila?"

"Dan, darling, what are you doing here?" The large-framed Benzium woman was dressed in a fluorescent yellow gown that floated around her in soft waves. Bright green hair sailed behind her as she engulfed him in her generous embrace.

"Carila, sweetheart. I would be honored if you would allow me to escort you into the casino." He did his best to extricate himself from her grasp, but she only clung to him tighter. Carila's servants milled around in a confused circle as the two friends spoke.

"Of course," Carila replied. "Darling, you look a mess. What have you been up to I wonder?"

"I apologize for my appearance." Dan took her arm, looping it through his own and led her up the stairs. Carila's servants fell into place around them, creating, as he'd hoped, a barrier between him and the goons. The entire entourage swept toward the casino.

After a few minutes spent aimlessly wandering, Carila whispered, "Dan, darling, exactly how many of these men are after you?"

"Oh, at least half a dozen, Caro, but don't let it worry you."

"I'm not worried, but back at the staircase, I did wonder if perhaps you could use some help."

Dan grinned. "How long were you watching?"

"Long enough."

Carila took the lead and pushed her way past various games tables and machines, giving Dan a brief respite. *How did the goons know?* They had purposely waited until after he'd opened the locker before they attacked.

Security was high in the locker bay. Clearly, they'd waited for an idiot to open the locker. Presumably because they didn't have a key. They had been ready for Toni. But how had they known about him? Someone had to be tracking the agent, someone who'd seen her hand him—the idiot—the key to the hottest storage compartment this side of the Sector One core. Dan figured those goons would do everything they could to stop him from getting back to Toni.

"I'm sorry Caro, sweetheart. I've got to go."

"Oh, of course, darling, but here. Let me help you." Carila turned with a flourish and knocked over a Kitek-elik waiter and his tray stacked high with multi-colored beverages. The pointy-eared waiter fell back onto his shell and the drinks he held cascaded to the ground around him.

"Oh my gods, you clumsy fool!" Carila cried, her voice carrying over the crowd. She spared Dan a wink before proceeding to blast the waiter for his clumsiness. Carila's attendants sprang to her side and within seconds the large woman's wailing had captured the attention of every gambler in the room. The area quickly milled with confused patrons and frantic staff doing their best to placate the boisterous wealthy woman.

Dan grinned at Carila's outrageous behavior. It was just the kind of scene his old friend loved to cause. He watched for a moment longer and then disappeared into the crowd.

*

"You had to open that door, didn't you?" Dan lectured himself and leaned back against the steelcrete wall cursing his bad luck. The cold emergency exit stairwell provided an excellent hiding place after having just escaped the ambush he—like an amateur—walked right into. His rapid reversal had dodged all but one shot fired his way. The laser bolt tore through his left shoulder. It throbbed angrily, reminding him of his stupidity with each beat of his heart.

He couldn't walk through the casino with a hole in his arm. Luckily, the flooring in this area of the casino was a rich ruby red and would disguise his trail. It gave him a few minutes to breathe before his attackers locked onto his location again.

Buzzing Toni, he reported his condition as he slid his jacket off. The agent's annoyance came through the comm clearly. Just like old times. Dan listened to the searchers thumping loudly in the hall outside. Waiting in place was not going to work.

He grit his teeth against the coming pain and sliced the tail of his shirt off with a small blade, wrapping the material tight around his arm. He could move his fingers and his wrist, but when he raised his arm, his shoulder throbbed in protest. Stifling a groan, he vowed not to do that again, eyed his jacket, and groaned again. He shrugged it on, in considerable pain and pulled the bag containing the locker's items over his head. *Gotta keep moving.*

Dan poked his head through the door and just as quickly ducked back. One of the goons stood right outside the door, only a few steps away. Dan waited until his pursuer disappeared into the room then moved into the corridor, pulled the door shut behind the goon and fired his pistol at the handle until it melted. The goon thudded against the door in fury. Dan took off for the casino proper and soon snaked his way amongst the numerous beginners Duilk and Chariji tables, squinting under the harsh casino lights. At last, he spied the exit.

About time. Dan ignored the cheers and screams that erupted around him as bells and buzzers filled the air. He moved unerringly toward the bright red sign. Behind him, a weapon charged.

Don't these guys ever give up? Humans and aliens alike screamed and ducked the zinging deadly blasts as they ran in all directions. The smart ones hid beneath tables as the number of shots increased. Through the hysterical mass, Dan could see the casino's guards heading his way. A red globe next to his head exploded. *Where the khegh-ing hell is Toni?*

Then he heard the most beautiful thing in the universe. "Stop sightseeing and get your butt up here." He looked up into Toni's eyes, grinned and hauled his ass into the hovercar. His gaze ran over Toni's disguise. "Nice dress."

*

LOCATION: Uxt – Gualliun System * Docking Bay 22 *
"Damn her," Dan muttered quietly as he stormed back to the *Renegade.*

The last barb Toni had flung at him as she'd kicked him off her ship had stung. *"You taught me not to trust you. You've got no one to blame but yourself."*

At least she had patched up his wound before she told him to get lost. Of course she hadn't forgiven him for leaving her behind on that moon. He'd been a fool to think his presence alone would change her mind. *I should have told her the truth.* The opportunity just hadn't presented itself, and once again it was too late.

Then again, he had been the one who'd lied to her. And then shot her. He wasn't sure how—or even if—he could make up for that. At the time, he'd had no choice.

"How'd it go with Agent Delle?" D'ena asked.

"Don't ask."

"That good, huh."

Back on the moon, after Toni had repaired his CII, D'ena had found Rycee's message, and leaving had been the only way to keep Toni safe. If she'd known about the killer, she'd never have let Dan leave the moon alone. The only way he'd figured he could stop her had been to make her so angry she wouldn't follow him. She didn't know he'd flown back after getting Rycee off his tail. He couldn't find her though. Somehow she'd already made it off the moon. She certainly didn't need him. He'd stopped looking for her after finding out she was back on the job. Figured it was smarter to stay out of her way. So why did he need her forgiveness? Why did he need her to know the truth? Twice now he'd had the chance to tell her and twice he'd failed.

She hated him, and he had the awful feeling his window with her had closed. It was too late to explain his reasons. She'd never believe him anyway. *Khegh it all.*

Dan ordered D'ena to scan the holonet for coded Cross contacts and disappeared into his quarters to brood.

He emerged when D'ena hollered for his attention. She had a priority message from Berni, Dan's ex-partner—work and otherwise.

"Dan, where the khegh are you? I've tried you four times and you know how I hate leaving messages. You're not dead, are you? Get your ass to Kyth-tact. It's in the Traynor system. I need your help.

The stunning woman's purple-eyed gaze narrowed. She ran both hands over her sweaty hair—the multi-colored strands looked murky when wet—and pushed it out of her eyes. She seemed stressed. It wasn't a good look on the sarcastic but usually calm woman.

"I took a job on Jantiea transporting a couple of crates, no questions asked, to a docking port on

Kyth-tact. You know me, I got suspicious. I mean, when the guy hired me, he said that under no circumstances was I to open any of the crates. Dan, it was a khegh of a lot of coin, you understand?

Yeah, he got that, in this life, it was all about the coin you made.

"*After I hit forcedspace, I opened 'em up. I found this. I didn't know, Dan, I swear I didn't. I know the rules.*

Berni held up a familiar-looking rifle. The same weapon he'd just fired in the casino during his and Toni's madcap escape. Class-four weaponry. It was one of the Cross's limited rules. No slaves. No class-four weaponry. No killing children. The light of the cargo bay reflected off the Resonator's control box. Berni lowered it and continued.

"*I can't take off and lay low, not with this batch on board. Besides, I'd like to know where these creeps got their hands on this kind of modified technology. I mean, there are a lot of crates, and they look specially designed. It's not the sort of patch-job you'd see between Sectors.*

"*I'll make the drop and put a tracer in one of the crates, work a little magic, turn on a little charm and see what I can find out.*

If this all goes ass-up, these blokes don't seem the type to accept a written apology, so get your butt here ASAP."

The woman broke off as muted alarms sounded around her. She looked up.

"Looks like I'm missing a party. Don't let me down, Dan. You owe me."

The screen went blank before it lit up again. D'ena's digital face scrunched in worry. "We'd better move if we want to get there in time to assist."

Dan swiveled in his chair. "Berni's not the type to sit around and wait for us to crash her party."

He and Berni had split their partnership years ago due to "competitive differences." Regardless, their parting had not been bitter and they still worked the occasional job together. Dan liked Berni—the smuggler was a real character. Fond of old pirate holofilms, she fancied herself quite the rebel against authority and preferred to take missions that enabled free trade to embargoed planets. She took particular joy in outsmarting the government agents sent to capture her.

Berni had a way of enticing attention and Dan was no exception. These days, he proclaimed immunity to her charms, but sometimes he wasn't so sure. Berni fascinated and frustrated him in equal measure. Shenghi, he had a problem. He constantly filled his life with impressive women who challenged him.

"How long since the message was received?" he asked.

"It was received at fifteen standard hours, recorded and sent six standard, four point seven six two one five half units approx."

"Thanks, De." It was more detail than he required, but despite her quirks, it told him what he needed to know. "We're already behind the deadline. Let's move." Dan initiated the *Renegade*'s booster sequence.

D'ena interrupted. "Boss, I'm getting a new message."

Hoping it was Berni, telling him to stand down and that she didn't need his help after all, he told the CII to put it on. D'ena was replaced by another familiar face. Dan grinned, "Jasmine, how are you?"

"Dan." Jasmine's stern expression sat him upright. Her ears flicked back. "Listen, this isn't a social call. I just received a message from a mutual friend. She's in trouble. The message was half-scrambled and a bit erratic."

"What did she say?" Jasmine must mean Berni. The Cross emergency communication system ordered a message for aid be sent to the ever watching eyes of the Cross's hidden operative, Jasmine. She retrieved and dispatched messages and collected information for all members. The Cross had no official leader—it was too dangerous. Besides, the group members detested orders and preferred to work alone. The only common thread was Jasmine. She also acted as co-ordinator for large-scale joint operations. No Cross member ever knew where she was based, for security purposes.

"It just said to get the message to you and to avoid the left ridge. I've got no idea what that means, but I assume you'll figure it out."

"I'll find her."

Jasmine smiled and her ears twitched. "When you do, remind her she owes me coin. I expect it soon, or I'll hack her account and retrieve it, along with a little extra in late fees."

"I'll let her know."

Jasmine signed off and Dan brought the main thrusters online. He lifted his ship clear of the dock. Berni would only have triggered the emergency system if she was in serious trouble. As the *Renegade* streaked across Uxt's sky, Dan spared a thought for the agent on the water planet below.

Toni had a slight reprieve but he'd be back. Whatever happened to Berni involved those damned Resonators. He intended to find out where they were being shipped and by whom. Toni was right about one thing—he did owe her. Without her help, he would never have got off that moon. He was going to help her now, whether she wanted it or not.

As he flew out of Uxt's atmosphere, he glanced down at the planet. *You'll see me again soon, Toni.*

*

LOCATION: Kyth-tact – Traynor System * Main Docking Port *

Dan flicked the catch securing his pistol to his belt and stepped off the *Renegade*'s lowered hatch. D'ena's words rattled around inside his head as he stalked away from the ship. "Berni's not the sort to cry wolverine, Boss. Watch your back. You know what those Resonators can do. These guys will be desperate to keep information about them to a minimum. They won't hesitate to get rid of anyone else involved."

Without glancing over his shoulder, the smuggler knew D'ena had closed the *Renegade*'s hatch and locked it tight against intrusion. He headed out. In Dan's vast experience, the only being who could tell him if Berni's Sunchaser was there would be the planet's dock master.

On descent to Kyth-tact's docking bay, Dan had avoided the left mountain ridge, just as Berni had warned, but scanned it curiously as he flew past. The ridge contained so many cannon emplacements hidden in the rock, he doubted the planet was anywhere near as uninteresting as he'd been led to believe. The delivery of anything to a place that looked like a more rundown version of a deserted town left him with a list of questions and no good answers.

The heat outside was oppressive, pressing down on him like he was in a dry sauna. Wouldn't want to stay out here for long. Dan ambled toward the master-house, keeping his expression calm and his body relaxed. Internally, his thoughts raced. *What happened to Berni? Why send Jasmine that emergency message?* She'd been under fire. He had seen that for himself. That she hadn't called to rescind the message gave him a cramp in his gut. Peering around the deserted bay, he couldn't figure out the reason for delivering Resonators here—unless this was not the weapons final destination.

"Delivery?" A woman inquired from the shadows of the master-house.

"Nope." Dan stopped dead in his tracks. He couldn't see the voice's originator. The top of Dan's head took the brunt of the sun's hot rays. The longer he stayed out in the open the more likely he'd burn.

"Something wrong with ya ship?"

"Nope," he answered without moving his hands.

"Then what in Xendia's name are ya doing in a dump like this?" A small, thick-bodied woman stepped from the shadows and grinned up at him, "Who ya looking for, kid?"

Dan grinned back. He'd been worried when the voice hadn't immediately revealed herself. "Not who, what. I'm looking for a Sunchaser, 'bout ten years old. Big bruise-type mark on the stern, seen it 'round?"

The woman shrugged. "Can't be sure, why?"

"Pilot owes me money, offered her ship as payment. Said she'd meet me here. I just have to find her."

The woman's grin grew broader. "Well now, you might just be in luck, pal. See, we've got an abandoned Sunchaser sittin' in the third bay, big bruise on her stern all right. I reckon that might be the one ya looking for."

Abandoned? "Where's the pilot?"

"Haven't seen her since she landed. She was with three big ugly blokes. Didn't look too friendly, mind ya. But ay, who her friends are is no concern of mine, you know what I'm saying? Landin' fee ran out this morning. Had no idea what to do with her 'til you came along. I'll sell it to ya."

"I want to look at her first." *Cheeky khegher. Ship's not even hers and she's already sold her.* Berni would be furious when she heard.

"Over here, pal."

He followed the woman from the hangar's shadow out into the inferno of sunshine. *Khegh, it's hot!* They stopped outside a building at the right of the landing strip. Stepping inside brought welcome relief from the heat. Dan stared at the ship in the pit. It was Berni's Sunchaser, all right. From casual observation, he could see scorch marks and laser burns along her hull.

"She the one ya lookin' for?"

"Yep."

Dan wandered down the stairs and over to the Sunchaser's damaged hatch. Looked like it had been forced open. "You wouldn't happen to know where the pilot went after she left, would you?"

"I don't … but old Mic might. Hang about." The woman turned toward the master-house and shouted, "Mic, get ya lazy ass out here!" She turned back to Dan. "He'll be right out." She walked away, leaving Dan alone with the *Tigerforce*.

Dan stepped onto the ramp. Footsteps sounded behind him. He whirled and drew his pistol, glaring down at the unknown man. "Mic?"

"Whatcha want?" The old feller rubbed his filthy hands with a stained rag. The deep lines in his skin shone with sweat.

Dan motioned toward the Sunchaser. "Seen the pilot?"

"Nup."

"See her when she first arrived?"

"Yep."

"Did she say where she was headed?"

"She weren't in no condition to say anything when I saw her. The three she was with said nothing as they carried her past neither."

Carried?

"Not pleased to be here, it seemed."

"Where did they go?" Dan asked.

"Didn't wanna get involved. I ain't seen nothing 'cept them draggin' her out of here and into bay eight."

"Eight, huh?" Dan glanced around. His skin twitched, like someone had drawn a bead on him. "Thanks." He climbed the Sunchaser's ramp, but before he entered, turned back to the old man to ask, "Can ya describe these three men?"

"One of 'em was huge, massive beard and covered in tats."

Dan nodded and entered his ex-partner's ship.

What a mess. He stepped gingerly over the broken remains of a number of bulkheads, and what looked like a door. Berni's ship had always been something of a mess—it was one of the reasons their partnership had ended when it had—but in the past, the mess had a logical madness to it. This was just mindless destruction. Stepping over a torn dressing gown and broken glass, Dan yanked at a buckled panel. The hole in the center said someone had fired point-blank into it. He examined the charred wiring with a studied eye. There was no way to fix this without at least a new C-nine chip.

Heaving a loud sigh, he peered around again. Given the state of the main room, he didn't hold out faith that the cockpit had been left untouched. *They tore off the door?* His gut churned as he stared at the cracked hinges, evidence of impatience and brute strength.

"Computer, recognize Daniel Colten. Code Seven Nine Beta, Berni Four." He wasn't sure the shipboard Computer Intelligence Interface would be operational. The outer security measures were kept on a separate system and Dan knew Berni had several ghost protection programs encrypted into her files. *Khegh it*, he'd shown her how to install most of them. With any luck, he might still be able to access the database. If Berni had any details on the Resonators, he could at least shoot that to Toni's CII while he looked for the missing smuggler.

"Accesss Graaaanted. Daaaniel Coltennn, Recognizzzed."

Piercing squeals tore through the cockpit as the *Tigerforce*'s CII sprang to life. Dan moved to the pilot's seat and stopped. The chair had been ripped right out of the floor. *Huh. Ain't that something.*

He popped open an access panel in the floor and tugged a handful of wires from within, stretching to twist the third foot off the seldom-used co-pilot's chair. The move released the small knife hidden in the arm. He started splicing. It was nice to know Berni hadn't changed all her hiding spots.

Eight minutes was all it took to jury-rig the system. When finished, he hoped to access the CII's memory core. It was another fifteen minutes to circumnavigate the security lockouts and overrides before he tried again. "Computer, initiate David program one."

"Please wait. Compiling. Complete." The distorted voice changed, becoming softer somehow. "Isss that you-you, Dan?"

"Yeah, Dave, it's me. The screens in here are shot to shenghi, you'll have to stick with audio. Run a self-diagnostic."

"What is …? Okay, h-a-a-ng on."

As the *Tigerforce*'s computer checked itself, Dan straightened up the cockpit in silence. He jumped when the CII spoke again. "Well. There you go. There are some sections of my code I cannot access and some that are jumbled enough to take years to read or repair by myself, but I appear functional."

"What happened?"

"I do not know. I am in the dark as much as you are."

Dan slumped to the floor. "She got a message off to Jasmine, so she could have planted something. We just have to find it."

"In my scan, I did not locate any additional code. She may have saved an entry as normal programming."

"Check for my name or Jasmine as part of the key."

"Searching … found."

"Can you play it?"

"It is fragmented but I can try. Audio only."

"No visual in here anyway, pal. Pipe it through."

Harsh static exploded into the room. "Dan ... you get this ... been tricked ... taken shipment ... would you believe the scarns have stormed my ship? They've got on board, but I've locked myself in the cockpit ... sent message to Jas ... tricked the scarns ... got hold of distrib ... on ... underground army amassing on ... plan to ..." The message became unintelligible under more static. Berni's voice crackled and became audible again. "Nail ... arns for me, Dan. They know I know and ... just say they ain't gonna be too ..." The message broke off after a final burst of static.

"Damn," Dan muttered.

"Second that," Dave agreed.

"You don't remember what happened?"

"There is nothing in my memory banks."

Dan stood up, shaking cockpit debris from his clothes. "I'll keep hunting. Look, I'll lock up as best I can, but I won't deactivate you. Give you a chance to repair some of the damage."

"Affirmative," Dave answered. As Dan left the cockpit, he heard the computer mutter, "Find her, Dan. Find her alive."

"Count on it," he promised.

After locking the hatch and re-initiating Berni's security measures, Dan headed toward bay eight. The place was deserted. No people, not even a sound of local wildlife. In the heat that rose off the cracked ground beneath his feet and the haze of the air in the distance, the cramping in his gut grew worse.

He poked his head around the doorframe of bay eight. It was empty, other than for the man he spoke to before. Mic stood in the center of the bay, waiting for him. Dan relaxed and stepped inside.

"This where they took her?"

"Who?"

"The Sunchaser's pilot." Dan spoke each word slowly and with precision so he wouldn't be misunderstood.

"Yep." Mic pointed a dirty, stubby hand toward a door off to the side of the bay. "Office over there."

Dan holstered his weapon and stepped inside before something flat and hard connected with his head. Pain exploded in the back of his skull, and he hit the ground, blacking out.

*

LOCATION: Midock * Docking Bay Behind Grand Senatorial House *

Concussion turned memories of his imprisonment on the Redflag ship into cheese. The holey kind. He did recall throwing up a lot. His head ached like the random strikes of tiny asteroids against his shields. A second concussion gained upon their loony escape had done a number on his short-term memory too.

He recalled the cell he'd been stuck in, Berni's voice and Toni's talking together—about him. Shenghi, he hoped he was remembering that wrong. There was also a slow jog through shipboard corridors, explosions, flashing lights and then that lumpy sofa on board Toni's ship as they flew to Midock.

Berni's expression told him he'd asked for the same details too many times already. It was concerning that he kept forgetting where they were. He and his ex-partner were currently scouring the lower level of the Grand Senatorial House—during a summit and important vote—surrounded by PST security and government guards while hunting for an assassin. He stared at Berni. "We're what now?" he asked.

"I'm not repeating it again. Get it together, Danny-boy, we don't have time for this."

"Toni's here?"

A sigh confirmed his question. "And we're searching for a shadowlink?"

"Balandez."

"We were on a Redflag—"

"Dan, I swear to Xendia, I will shoot you if you keep asking. We were held prisoner by some nutjob named Gallian. Your ex-girlfriend—the crazy agent—helped us escape, so now we're helping her save the Vice-President's life."

"Ramo is in danger?"

"Khegh it, Dan."

He held up his hands. "Sorry. It's just … how are we …? How have we not been arrested? Smugglers at a political shindig?"

"Agent's protection. Look, would you shut it? We're looking for a ghost. A deadly one. Let's not advertise we're out here looking, huh? Ever heard of stealthy?"

He mimed zipping his lips.

A crackly voice burst from Berni's commdisk. "The boss has found the shadowlink." That sounded a lot like Toni's CII.

Berni glanced at Dan. "Oh, thank khegh."

Dan sagged and Berni caught him. "Come on, let's get you back to the ship. The agent's got it covered now. We gotta split before Ramo sends the guard after us."

"You said—"

"Everything just changed. Delle doesn't need us anymore."

Wasn't that always the way. She didn't need him. "She might still … don't we have immunity?"

"Khegh it, Danny-boy! Tone—Antonio Zaambuka— her boss—negotiated the immunity with Jas and your Toni will uphold it sure, but the rest of these security agents will see our rap sheet first, shoot second and read the deal last. You hear me? The shadowlink's here to kill the VP. We need to go now before they lock everything down."

With Berni's assistance—hoisting Dan's weight over her shoulders—they made their way into the landing bay. "Her ship?" Berni asked with a grin.

"Let's not push it," he told her.

Berni pointed to a two-person shuttle. "Should we leave a note?" Her eyes glittered with humor, despite the strain of carrying Dan.

Dan smirked. He glanced at the door leading back into the government house. "She dropped the bounty? Five months reprieve?"

"Interesting woman. Dan, I never figured you for stupid, but leaving her behind all those years ago? You're stupid."

"Not now." He watched Berni pop the access panel and hack the shuttle's security system. Alarms burst to life, filling the parking dock. He glanced up, an automatic reaction to alarms. "Khegh."

"She'll survive, Dan. You'll see her again."

"Of course. She's impossible to kill."

Berni tied the tangled wires together as fast as her fingers allowed. "Come on." A hard punch to the panel had the shuttle's door sliding open.

"I'll have to remember your advanced code-cracking technique," Dan told her.

"Your shuttle awaits."

Together, they stumbled up the ramp and dropped into the pilots' seats. That was the entirety of the shuttle. Passenger seats in the back, pilots' seats in the front. It gleamed white and tan—a fancy politician's shuttle.

Berni initiated all the sequences she could find and fired the shuttle's thrusters. Exhaustion made Dan dizzy. He closed his eyes. "Where're we headed?"

"Back to Kyth-tact. Once we retrieve our ships, I've got an idea for our next hit."

Dan dragged one eye open to peer at his ex-partner as she operated the shuttle's controls. He wondered how Toni was faring. "Yeah?"

"I know the destinations of some of those rifles. How about we go crash a party or two?"

"You know where they went?" Dan huffed out a laugh and closed his eyes, waving his hand around. So he *could* still help Toni. Put some good faith in the bank so to speak. He could still find a time to talk to her. When the timing was better.

Dan could see the need for revenge in Berni's eyes. They were agreed then. He rubbed his head, gingerly feeling the painful lumps. Once again, he was taking off and leaving the agent behind.

Maybe it was for the best. She was perfectly capable of handling things without him around. She didn't need him, but did she *want* him? Perhaps he just needed to apologize and let things lay where they ended up? "Let's go," he muttered.

For the first time in all their history working together, Berni obeyed his order without complaint.

*

LOCATION: Restick Seven – Caldoorh System

The night was silent. An unnatural quiet. No moon lit the sky, no star illuminated the oppressive black. Storm-filled cloud cover stretched overhead as far the eye could see. A heavy feeling of anticipation pervaded every building, every tree, and every breath. A storm was coming. You could feel it electrifying every hair, reverberating through every heightened heartbeat.

Two figures ran for their lives. Behind them, a large stone warehouse exploded into an enormous wall of flames. Pieces of stone, metal and steelcrete were thrown high into the air, glowing red against the black of the night and cascading to the ground around them in a deadly shower.

Berni slowed to a gallop and glanced over her shoulder to watch the show. Dan dropped his pace to level with her. "You said you wouldn't plant as many explosives this time."

"I got a little carried away," she said unapologetically, shrugging her slim shoulders.

Several smaller explosions shook what was left of the warehouse's foundations as the Resonators' power packs exploded.

Dan stopped running to watch the fire destroy the building. Flame and smoke turned the thunderous sky from shadowed indigo to molten red. Lightning ripped the clouds apart and, an instant later, they were soaked to the skin. Thunder roared and the rain fell harder.

"Next one?" Berni screamed over the sound of the storm.

"Send the list to the PST," he yelled back. "They can deal with what's left. We need to lay low for a while."

Both smugglers had cheered the announcement of the new government's formation, while complaining that things would never be the same.

It had been good to know Toni had succeeded in her mission to save the Vice-President and thus the entire peace summit.

"Oh, but I'm having so much fun." Lightning danced across the sky in a show that rivaled the explosions on the ground. Almost. "What'll I do now?"

"I'm sure we can think of something," he told her.

"We?"

"Why not?"

She squinted at him. "And the agent?"

"I'm thinking I need a new plan."

"Ha!" Dan's smoke-streaked friend grinned wickedly and led the way into the trees.

His thoughts were not on their next move, however, but on a certain agent. He would find her again soon. They needed to talk. Seeing Toni, working with her, had reignited the feelings he'd pushed aside in his rush to escape Rycee's tightening grip. He had four months left of an official clemency to do something about it. He had to make this right. And maybe, *maybe*, he would see where they stood.

These last few weeks had shown they were able to work together. They were good together and he hoped she would want to hear his truth.

I'll see you soon, Toni.

EXCERPT FROM *WHITE FIRE: A TONI DELLE ADVENTURE*

The sun set, and the city woke up hungry.

As the lights of the metropolis brightened, shadows crept into alleyways and emerged from dark corners, ready to conduct activities that should never see the light of day. In the heart of this darkness, evil held its breath.

Toni squinted into the murky alley light, straining to make out any detail around her. Warm blood trickled down her face. Her bruised ribcage ached with every breath she took, and luckily—or unluckily, depending on the point of view—no startled pedestrian had yet stumbled into the alley.

Of the two men standing before her, she would have to watch the Tarrelian carefully. Her heart raced as she took in his muscular frame and giant arms.

Towering over her by at least a head, he glared through tiny eyes. His face looked like he'd taken several beatings, leaving him with a flat nose and misshapen jaw. She'd caught a glimpse of the Kilmarc tattoo on his wrist with its distinctive green spiral barely exposed below the cuff of his sleeve. It was the mark of a gun for hire, and when she stared into his expressionless eyes, she knew she was in trouble. Sweat broke out across the back of her neck. He would kill her without qualm.

The Tarrelian had called the other man Tubby. The first time she'd heard it, she'd laughed, given the excess body weight the man carried. She wasn't laughing now. He scowled at her through dull watery blue eyes. Her gaze flicked over his rumpled clothes. He'd probably lived in them for the last few days. That was how long she'd been hunting him.

Tubby shuffled from one foot to the other, one hand outstretched over the killer's wrist, as if he could actually stop the man from shooting her. She wasn't hopeful he'd show any mercy. Tubby needed her seal and the chip warrant for his arrest if he was to escape the spaceport's security cordon, and he could only get that if she was alive to print it, hence the tense standoff. Her stare returned to the trained killer.

At times like this, she regretted her choice in career.

Tubby stepped out from behind his beady-eyed bodyguard and grinned. "So, you're Agent Delle?"

From her periphery, Toni saw his eyes drop to travel the length of her body, pausing at her empty holster and missing agent's star. Her skin crawled at the lingering leer.

"You're a freaky looking one, that's for sure."

She didn't take her eyes off the Tarrelian, watching for the slightest twitch. Forcing her breathing to remain steady took more concentration than she could spare, but like the Tarrelian, she remained poker-faced.

Tubby shuffled into her view, his grin faded. "Did you think I'd let anyone catch me, especially a PST Agent?" He sneered when she didn't respond. With a shake of his head, he turned to the hired gun and spat, "Just lemme get the contract, and *then* you can get rid of her. Leave nothing to link me to any of this. If other agents suspect she's been murdered, they won't ever stop looking for me, ya hear?"

The Tarrelian didn't answer. His finger tightened on the trigger. Toni tensed.

"For Xendia's sake, don't do it here! I said get the contract first! If Gallian finds out, I'm a dead man." Tubby hissed, grabbing at the gunman's arm.

Gallian?

The Tarrelian stared blankly at his client's hand, and Tubby removed it slowly. Toni shifted her weight.

"Better do it here. It'll look like a beggar with a khegh load of luck killed her." The Tarrelian's voice sounded rough and scratchy, as though he didn't use it often.

Shuffling back, Toni pressed up against a barrier of rotted wooden boards, hoping to feel them move, but they made a solid wall, preventing her escape. Her gaze flew in every direction beneath her electronic shades. The alley was located behind a cheap rundown bar called The Dockyard. It was the sort of place one might frequent when down on their luck, working two jobs to keep a family alive and needing to get away for just a little while. She had no faith she'd be saved by the untimely appearance of a bar patron.

Khegh it! If someone did appear, it wasn't as though they would help her. People just didn't do that. Besides, the alley dead-ended only a few yards from her current position. Crates stacked haphazardly against the brick wall opposite looked like they'd always been there. The overflowing dumpster at the mouth of the alley smelled like it had never been emptied. Ever. And above her head was an unreachable metal ladder. It disappeared up into darkness but that didn't much matter. Her breathing quickened with the realization she was trapped. She swallowed, her mouth too dry to generate much in the way of saliva. *I need a distraction.*

Blinking rapidly, she flicked through the display settings of her tinted glasses, finding nothing until she scanned the area with the X-ray setting. The crates were empty.

A low growl rumbled out of the shadows behind Tubby. The Tarrelian twisted his head sharply.

About time, partner. Toni threw herself at the pile of crates. The gunman fired as the crates tumbled down around her. The growl increased in volume. Toni darted up, her fingers wrapped around the neck of an empty bottle. A large shadow propelled itself from the darkness. A glint of sharp teeth flashed before Mate roared into the Tarrelian's face and chomped down on his weapon, including the hand holding it.

The man cried out and dropped the pistol. He shook his arm, but her trusty C-bot locked his jaws and would not be dislodged.

Tubby stumbled back. Small whimpers ghosted from his open mouth. Mate's growls deepened as he dragged the Tarrelian to the ground.

Scrambling to her feet, Toni threw the bottle at Tubby's fat head and dove for the Tarrelian's fallen pistol. Tubby ducked, the bottle shattering against the wall, and launched himself at the weapon. He got his fingers to it, Toni knocked it out of his reach. They hit the ground hard. She wrenched her head away as Tubby swung the pistol up and fired. The laser bolt hit dirt mere inches from her ear.

Close. She grabbed at the pistol again. A scream punctured the air behind them, distracting Tubby and letting Toni wrench the weapon from his hands. She pushed the overweight man off and climbed unsteadily to her feet. A burst of laser fire caught the Tarrelian right between his beady little eyes. As he collapsed, Mate spun and howled, shattering the sudden silence. He stalked toward Toni. Tubby fainted.

"Will you cut that out?"

The howl broke off as the C-bot sat. It was now fully dark. Toni blinked to engage her night vision display and examined the familiar shaggy canine shape.

"What took you so long?"

Mate scratched at his ear with a hind leg. "Well, I assumed you had everything under control."

"Yeah, I had them right where I wanted them." At the C-bot's snort of disbelief, she laughed. "Your timing is impeccable." Raising her hand to the corner of her mouth she examined the sticky residue. *Damn it.* Searching her pockets for a cloth to wipe the blood away, she muttered, "Did you hear that? Gallian." She snatched her pistol from the dead man's belt and shoved it into her holster. "What took you so long, anyway?"

Mate growled. "It is a long run. How did he get the drop on you, Boss?"

"He just did, that's all." Toni was tired. It had nearly cost her life. *I need a break.* She felt no elation over closing this case but with Tubby's arrest, her current mission was over. *Just don't mention Gallian. Ask for a break … No, demand one.* The invitation she received this morning popped into her mind. Yes, a holiday would be perfect. Then she could confirm her attendance at the game. A final dab at the blood on her face and she shoved the red-stained rag back into her pocket.

Brushing alley dust off her pants she ordered. "Call this in. But, uh, neglect to mention You Know Who."

Mate would send a high frequency message to Zach, who would then forward the message via forcedspace relays onto Agent headquarters.

Toni wanted a bath. She also had to call Jas back and confirm the date, and she had to get her money from Zaambuka, all while making sure he didn't assign her a new case. She spied a smudge on her pristine white shirt. Her eyes narrowed. In one move, she grabbed Tubby by the front of his shirt and hauled him to his feet. She didn't have much to call her own—her C-bot, her ship and her clothing—but she looked after what was hers. She shook him until he regained consciousness.

The gun-runner's watery gaze focused on her. "Look, Delle, don't be angry about the Kilmarc. I hired him to protect my interests. With your reputation d-do you blame me? Huh?" Tubby glanced at the bloody body. "Obviously, he's not as fast as you. I mean, he's dead, isn't he? All you have is a bloody lip and a dirty shirt—" Toni pushed him hard into the brick wall.

"Do you know," she began softly, "how much this shirt cost? It's pure rainsilk. I got it on Jamith-phi. It's tailormade. Do you know how much time and money went into its creation?" She slammed the criminal into the wall again. He had no idea how necessary the silk was to protecting her skin.

"Listen, Delle, I'll buy you a new one. By Xendia herself, I'll buy you six. Just let me go and y-you'll get them by next week."

"Good try. Ten points for effort. But contrary to what you might have heard, I don't take bribes. Just cold, hard coin from my boss after I turn you in." *Don't ask him, don't ask.* "How is Gallian connected to this?" *Khegh it!*

His face paled. She worried he was going to faint again. She grabbed his arms. "Well?"

"Who?"

"The guns. Were they for Gallian?"

He shook his head. "I don't know no Gallian. The guns are mine."

She huffed out a sigh and gestured with a finger for him to turn around. He searched her face and complied. She cuffed him a little harder than she needed to.

"Hey, that hurts!"

"That's for my shirt. Now shut up," she said shoving him toward the alley's end. Mate fell into place beside her. Exhaustion weighed heavily; her muscles ached in places they weren't supposed to. She stretched her eyes wide and shook her head. *Yeah, I need a break.*

Tubby glanced down at the huge animal with fear-filled eyes. Mate snarled, exposing his sharp, white teeth.

"Now, don't do anything stupid, will you? Otherwise my friend here may decide he wants to play fetch with parts of you." Toni leaned close to Tubby and whispered, "He sounds kinda playful, doesn't he?"

Tubby whimpered.

READ IT NOW …

ACKNOWLEDGMENTS

I'd like to thank the following people without whom this collection would not have happened. I hope you have enjoyed reading them as much as I have enjoyed writing them.

Anthony, Cathy and Bernadette—you know why.

Hayley, Stefanie, Lisa, Jen, Kat, Justine, Blair and Cat, Brigitte, Laura, Madelyn, Amin and Lucy. Thank you for your support!

Nanna and Poppa. Miss you, Pop.

Linh, my lovely, lovely friend. You rock! Your endless support gives me strength. Thank you for reading

White Fire in all its lifecycles and for believing in my crazy idea of putting together a collection of POV short stories. I believe in us. One day, we will be signing our books together, side by side!

Margo and Carolyn, thank you for reading it over and over, and for your CP & Beta-ery goodness! You keep me sane and you keep me going. Every time I receive an email from you, my writing becomes better. You are just fabulous. Keep on keeping on. I can't wait to read your words soon.

The Friday Fictioneers Community, thank you!

Mum and Dad, for your endless support. I couldn't do this if you didn't believe in me.

Kit Carstairs, Stuart MacDonald, Marissa Fuller, Kate Foster, Joel Naoum and Rebecca Hamilton—you make my words sing! Thank you for everything.

To Libby Turner. You made this happen. Your suggestion over wine and gossip started me thinking about pulling this madness together. Thank you! You are an amazing editor who just *gets* my crazy brain. Here's to the next Toni Delle Adventure!

To James and the team at Dymocks Knox City. Thank you for supporting local authors! I really appreciate everything that you do.

To Helen, for still believing in my writing.

To Gerry, for loving me and listening to my endless doubts, changes, thoughts, edits, complaints, dreams, desires, hopes and fears. And for keeping me going when I want to chuck in the towel.

I love you all so much. Thank you!

Laurie Bell

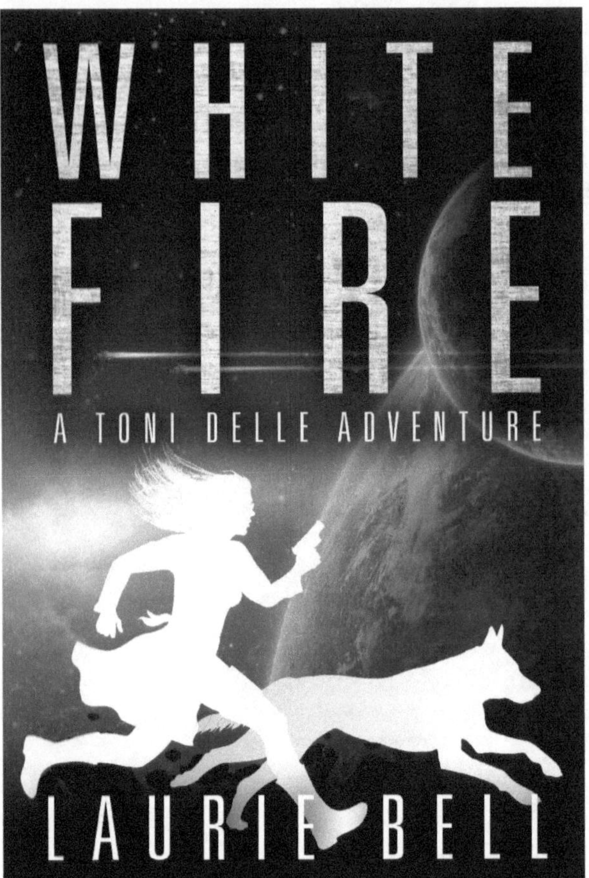

WHITE
FIRE
A TONI DELLE ADVENTURE
LAURIE BELL